TIGHTROPE

TIGHTROPE

gillian cross

OXFORD
UNIVERSITY PRESS

OXFORD
UNIVERSITY PRESS

Great Clarendon Street, Oxford OX2 6DP

Oxford University Press is a department of the University of Oxford.
It furthers the University's objective of excellence in research, scholarship,
and education by publishing worldwide in

Oxford New York

Auckland Cape Town Dar es Salaam Hong Kong Karachi
Kuala Lumpur Madrid Melbourne Mexico City Nairobi
New Delhi Shanghai Taipei Toronto

With offices in

Argentina Austria Brazil Chile Czech Republic France Greece
Guatemala Hungary Italy Japan Poland Portugal Singapore
South Korea Switzerland Thailand Turkey Ukraine Vietnam

Oxford is a registered trade mark of Oxford University Press
in the UK and in certain other countries

British Library Cataloguing in Publication Data

Data available

ISBN: 978-0-19-275589-6
1 3 5 7 9 10 8 6 4 2

Printed in Great Britain
Paper used in the production of this book is a natural,
recyclable product made from wood grown in sustainable forests.
The manufacturing process conforms to the environmental
regulations of the country of origin.

To Kaby

1

Ashley stopped at the traffic lights on the Row, looked across the road—and saw the best wall in the world.

And it had been there all her life.

Jabbing her elbow into Vikki's ribs, she raised her eyebrows and nodded over the road, towards Fat Annie's and the chippie. Vikki followed where she was looking, and her eyebrows almost disappeared into her hair.

'Ash! You *can't!*'

'Sssh!' Ashley hissed. 'Shut up.' They were on their way home from school, and there were other people all round them.

Vikki shut up, but her eyes were like marbles as the lights changed and they crossed the Row. She couldn't stop looking up at the wall.

It was a big, blank space, where Fat Annie's rose a whole storey higher than the chippie next door. The top of the side wall was exposed, and there was nothing on it at all. Not a mark. It was just waiting for someone to get up there and tag it. And all you'd have to do was climb on to the roof of the chippie and walk along.

Twenty feet up in the air, in full view of the Row. With nothing to stop you if you fell.

1

'You can't!' Vikki whispered again, when they reached the other side of the road. 'Ash, you're mad. You'll kill yourself.'

'Be quiet!' Ashley growled, looking over her shoulder. She didn't want anyone else getting there first.

But it wasn't that easy to make Vikki give up. She grabbed Ashley's arm and shook it. 'Listen to me—'

'There's nothing to say.' Stubbornly Ashley ignored her, heading sideways, into Fat Annie's. 'Got to pick up some cheese.'

She had to push her way in. The place was full of kids scrabbling round the counter with chocolate and chewing gum, trying to barge in front of each other. Fat Annie's eyes were everywhere—on the shop door, flicking up at the security camera, and checking every coin she was offered—and as her fingers banged away at the till, she was bellowing at the queue-jumpers.

'Get back and wait your turn. Dean Fox! And you, Shorty! And watch your language, or I'll be round to talk to your mother.'

Ashley pushed through the crowd, heading for the cheese counter and trying to lose Vikki in the scrum. But Vikki was right on her heels, still banging on about the wall.

'Ash, you've got to listen! You'd be crazy to—'

Ashley ignored her and began burrowing in the cheese cabinet, hunting for a bit of cheap Cheddar. Vikki leaned closer, to whisper in her ear.

'You'll fall! You'll break your legs! And even if you don't, someone's going to catch you. It'll be a disaster.'

'I can handle it,' Ashley said. 'Now be quiet. I don't want everyone to—'

Out of the corner of her eye, she caught a movement. She glanced up and stopped dead. The Hyena was marching across the shop towards them, like the US Cavalry riding over the horizon.

That wasn't typical. Usually, he was the opposite of his mother. Where Annie yelled and bullied the customers, the Hyena crept around, turning his soft pasty face away from people's eyes. He slunk round the shop like a hyena with its tail between its legs—if a hyena can be going bald on top.

He wasn't slinking today, though. He was heading straight for Vikki, looking fierce and determined. But she hadn't realized yet. Ashley struggled not to laugh.

'You'd better let me alone,' she murmured. 'It looks as if I'm going to be rescued.' Then she fluttered her eyelids pathetically and whimpered, 'Please leave me alone.'

At first, Vikki thought it was a joke and she bared

her teeth, pretending to snarl. Then she realized that Ashley was serious and she whipped round.

By then, the Hyena was just behind her. He looked at Ashley. 'Is she bothering you?'

Vikki didn't give Ashley a chance to reply. She leaned back against the cheese counter and looked at the Hyena with bold, bright eyes. 'How could I bother anyone?' she drawled.

Then she hitched up her skirt—the last possible centimetre—and took a step towards him. The Hyena stepped backwards, nervously, and she grinned and strolled past him, to the magazine shelves. Standing on tiptoe, she reached down a copy of *Penthouse* and began to flick through the pages.

The Hyena's pale face turned pink.

He was hesitating on the brink of saying something, but Annie got there first. She screamed at him, all the way across the shop.

'Geoffreeee! Don't let the children at the men's magazines!'

Immediately, everyone in the queue turned to look. Vikki grinned again and raised the magazine higher, and Ashley bent over the cheese, trying not to laugh.

The Hyena couldn't bring himself to look directly at Vikki, but he reached out a long arm to take the magazine away. His bony hands were shaking faintly, the way they always did. Vikki pretended not to notice. Whisking the magazine out of his reach, she turned her back and went on looking through it.

Fat Annie yelled at the top of her voice, as she rang in a couple more Mars Bars and three bags of crisps. '*Geoffreeee*! Come on the till!'

Even from the far end of the shop, Ashley could feel the Hyena's relief. He turned away from Vikki and scuttled to the counter to take his mother's place, and Annie lumbered out, heading for the magazine rack.

Vikki wasn't stupid. By the time Annie got there, she was reading *Mizz* and her skirt had dropped to its full length. But that didn't make any difference to Annie. She tweaked the magazine away and jerked her head at the door.

'Outside, madam.'

Vikki was beaten, but not squashed. She sauntered to the door, saying 'Hi,' to everyone in the queue and rolling her eyes at the Hyena. Ashley grinned to herself and went on with her cheese hunt.

When she finally decided which piece she could afford, the queue had vanished. Fat Annie was still by the magazine rack, tidying it up with brisk, angry fingers, and the Hyena was alone at the counter. He took Ashley's cheese and looked sideways at her, flicking his tongue over his lips.

'How's your mother coming along, then?'

Why did people always ask that? She gave him her standard plastic smile.

'She's fine, thanks.'

Flick, went the Hyena's tongue again. Flick, flick. He made Ashley feel clammy all over. She dropped her money on to the counter, avoiding his hand, and got out of the shop as fast as she could.

Vikki was waiting outside, ready to start up about the wall again, but Ashley didn't give her a chance.

'*No!*' she said. 'OK?'

'But—'

'Look, Vik, you don't really think you're going to change my mind, do you?'

Vikki thought about it for a moment and then shrugged. 'OK, so you're pig-headed. But you *are* going to fall, you know. One day.'

'That's my lookout.' Ashley dropped the cheese into her pocket and swung her bag on to her shoulder. 'You just wait until tomorrow, and see what that wall's like.'

Vikki put her head on one side. 'There's other ways of getting kicks, you know. You could come to the party tonight, instead. With me and Matt.'

'I'm a bit busy tonight,' Ashley muttered. 'But— thanks.'

It was what she always said, but she was pleased to be asked. Vikki always asked her, even though she got the same answer every time. Ashley smiled at her.

'Hope it's a good party, though. Be nice to Matt.'

'I'll be so nice he'll think it's his birthday.' Vikki closed her eyes dreamily. 'Wait and see what *he's* like tomorrow. He'll be dancing on air.'

She waved a hand and floated away down the Row. *As if*, Ashley thought. Things were never straightforward with those two. Matt was twice Vikki's size, but she'd got him on a lead, and she could never resist wrapping it round his neck. There was bound to be some drama or other to sort out at school tomorrow.

The wall was a whole lot simpler than all that stuff.

Ashley walked round the corner, into Railway Street, where she lived, but she wasn't heading home. Not yet. She was going to spy out the ground.

Immediately behind the shops there was a little service road, running parallel to the Row. She glanced round and then strolled into it. To work out how to get on to the roof of the chippie.

GEOFFREY

You always have a favourite, don't you? In any crowd of people, there's one who catches your eye. There must be hundreds of schoolchildren who come into the shop, but Ashley's my special one. She's neat and tidy, for a start. And quiet. And she looks so—It's that fair hair and those big blue eyes, I suppose. She's always stood out from the others. Even before I knew about her.

But when you know about her life—well, it's like a fairy tale, isn't it? The other children come in pushing and shoving, grabbing for chewing gum and Cokes, and they've got more money than they know what to do with. Ashley always buys real food. Eggs and cheese. Milk and flour and margarine. And you can see her checking the prices.

I didn't understand at first. I thought she was just doing the shopping to help her mother out. I didn't know that she does a lot more than the shopping. Not until Mrs Macdonald told me.

I don't like to gossip, of course. It gets the shop a bad name. But once I knew about Ashley I kept my ears open and it's wonderful what you pick up if you stay quiet and listen. Little bits here and there. Things she says to the other children, and odd remarks people make. I know all about her now. Where she lives. The date of her birthday. Where she goes to school. Lots of things.

I get really angry when I see other children pestering her. Like that girl today. You can see what she's like, with that short skirt and dyed hair. She's a—Well, I

8

don't like to say it, but it's obvious, isn't it? It makes me feel sick just seeing her talking to Ashley.

And Ashley's so good about it. You could tell she was being bullied, but she didn't fuss. When I saw her looking up, I thought—I know it was silly, but I couldn't help it—I thought I wish I could protect her.

It's not fair, the sort of life she has to live. Not when you think about someone like Eddie Beale. He never does a stroke of work, and he has it all. When Ashley comes in looking tired and worried, I wish I could scoop up an armful of luxury items and drop them into her basket. 'Take these, my dear,' I'd say, 'for being such a good customer.'

I'd give her frozen rump steak, and petit pois. Fruits of the forest cheesecake and extra thick double cream. She deserves the very best. Sometimes, when I see her with her baked beans and pork luncheon meat, my hands actually ache with wanting to snatch extra things off the shelves.

But it wouldn't do, of course. Mother would have a fit, to begin with. And the other customers wouldn't like it. So I have to make do with giving her that extra bit of attention, to help her feel good.

I always smile and ask how her mother's doing. She never says much, but I know she appreciates it. This is a rough, difficult neighbourhood, and everyone's in a hurry. There aren't many sensitive people around. I *like to think that she looks on this as a special place, where she has a true friend. Someone quiet and gentle and considerate, who understands her and what she has to put up with.*

I hope she'd come to me if she was ever in trouble. I'd look after her.

2

Ashley stood in the alley behind Fat Annie's and looked up at her wall. It wasn't going to be easy. But she could manage it. She *knew* she could.

First, she had to get into the yard behind the chippie. All the shops had yards at the back, surrounded by brick walls topped with broken glass or barbed wire. The chippie's had broken glass, and it didn't look too threatening. Her bit of blanket would take care of that.

Inside the yard, the real climbing began. The chippie had a single-storey extension, sticking out at the back. She reckoned she could shin up the drainpipe at the corner of that. The real problem was getting on to the main roof. That was going to be fingertip stuff. She'd have to use the window ledges and put a foot on the guttering.

If it was strong enough.

She narrowed her eyes, trying to see how good the brackets were. They looked pretty solid, and the gutter was cast iron. She reckoned she could make it. Then she could crawl up the slope of the roof.

After that, it was a tightrope walk. Four or five metres along the ridge of the roof. If she kept her balance, she'd be fine. If not—curtains. She'd go pitching down into the yard, or into the Row on the far side. It wouldn't take much. Just a loose tile, or a slip in her concentration.

She looked up at the ridge and felt her whole body come to life.

And now, the beautiful Miss Cindy will risk her life to bring you a daredevil display of balance and courage! Watch her climb to the roof, without a safety net!! Thrill to her death-defying ridge walk!!! Marvel at her calmness as she leaves her signature on this IMPOSSIBLE WALL!!!!

She was going to do it all right. She knew it, in her bones.

A second later, she was strolling out of the alley again, thinking about time. Three in the morning ought to be safe enough. There was no one around then except people like Spider Mo. Deadheads. She could get away with anything then, as long as she planned it right.

As she went home, she worked out all the details. That was how she'd done so many great walls without being spotted. Planning. She was hardly aware of how slowly she was going. Not until she reached the front door, and realized that she was half an hour later than usual.

Her mother was already shouting as she walked in.

'What time do you call this? You've been out of

12

school for an hour! You know I won't have you hanging around like that. You'll get into all sorts of trouble.'

Here we go. Ashley hung her bag on the end of the banisters and walked into the front room letting the shouting wash over her. Pauline was sitting on the bed, and she was white and shaking with fury.

'You knew I was all on my own here! You're just taking advantage. If you don't get in on time, I'll have to come and look for you . . . ' Her breathing was already getting rougher. 'What do you think it's like for me? Sitting here and waiting? You don't care, do you? You're stupid and lazy and self-centred . . . '

The only thing to do was think of it as a storm. Ashley had worked that out long, long ago. Sit it out and then see if there's any real damage. She thought about rocks and lighthouses. Strong things that could take a battering.

Pauline thumped her fist on to the bed. It was a sad, soft sound, muffled by the blankets.

'Just because I'm not too good at the moment, you think . . . '

Ashley bent her head and let the words wash over her.

'You wait until I'm a bit better! Then you'll see . . . '

Her mother's face was hectic pink now. The words

she was shouting were as fragile as smoke. If she panted any harder, her gasps would blow them away.

'Answer me!' Pauline shouted. 'Why don't you ever answer? I hate it when you go blank like that! You're so . . . so . . . so . . . '

That was it. The pink flush on her face drained away and the words dissolved in a fit of coughing. Ashley went across the room and sat down on the bed.

'It's all right,' she said. She put her arm round Pauline's shoulders and began to chant. 'Don't panic. Just breathe and breathe and breathe. And breathe. And breathe . . . '

She kept it up until her mother's body took over the rhythm, and the dreadful juddering breaths slowed down. And down. And down. Until, for one calm moment, they sat together, breathing at the same speed. Perfectly still.

Then Pauline pulled away and put her hands over her face.

'I'm sorry. Oh, I'm sorry, Ash.'

'It's all right,' Ashley said. 'I was only getting some cheese, you know.' She stood up quickly, but she couldn't get away before Pauline started.

'No, it's not all right. I'm a lousy mother. It's no life for you. You should be out with your friends. You ought to be having a good time—'

Ashley hated that. It was worse than the shouting.

'I'll make some tea,' she said. And she went through to the kitchen.

Normally Pauline was in bed by ten o'clock. But it took her a long time to calm down after one of her storms. It was nearly midnight before Ashley finished helping her on with her nightdress. Pauline was very thin and everything had to be done carefully, in case she bruised. She had taken two hours to eat her share of the cauliflower cheese, and then she'd brought half of it up again. Ashley had said, *It doesn't matter* and *It's all right* so often that she thought her tongue would drop out.

By the time they shuffled across the front room to the bed, it was ten to twelve. On good days, Pauline could walk with just an arm to lean on, but that night Ashley was half carrying her.

Pulling the covers back, she lowered her mother carefully, to sit on the bed. Then she picked up the hairbrush and began to brush Pauline's long, brown hair, teasing out the tangles with her fingers.

'I ought to have it all cut off!' Pauline said suddenly. Viciously. 'It's just another job for you to do, isn't it?'

Ashley's fingers didn't falter. 'It's all right. I don't mind. You look nice with it long.'

Pauline took a strand between her fingers. 'I'll manage it myself tomorrow. Really I will. It's just . . . I'm so tired tonight.'

'It's all right,' Ashley said again, plaiting the hair with quick, practised fingers. 'I'll send you a bill tomorrow. Slave driver.'

Pauline relaxed and let her finish the plait. Then she lay back in bed and let Ashley pull up the duvet round her shoulders. Ashley gave her plait a tweak.

'Sleep well.'

'And you. Don't sit up.'

'I won't,' Ashley said.

She didn't. She went upstairs and changed into her leggings and her black sweatshirt. Then she lay flat on her bed and started to think about what she was going to put on Fat Annie's wall.

Pauline started snoring at twenty-five past one. In a couple of minutes, the sounds were steady and regular. Ashley waited another hour, to let the streets clear, and then slipped off the bed and took her spray-cans out of the chest of drawers. Four of them this time. Black, red, orange, and yellow.

She wrapped them in rags, to stop them clinking, and pushed them into her rucksack, with a piece of old blanket bundled on top. Then she crept downstairs and into the kitchen. Very carefully, she opened the back door.

She had done it so often she could manage in the pitch dark. One step down into the garden. Close the door. Then six steps to the fence.

She felt her way down to the loose board and slipped through into Mrs Macdonald's garden. That was safe enough. Mrs Macdonald was always in bed by eleven. The dangerous part came on the other side, when she let herself out into the alley. It was a narrow, arched space between Mrs Macdonald's and the rest of the terrace. A good place for drunks.

She was in luck today. There was no one there except a very old man, flat out on his back. She stepped over him and edged out of the alley into the street. It was completely empty. Like a shadow, she slipped up the road in her old trainers.

Behind the shops, the service road was very dark, but that was good. She could be invisible. Padding along to the chippie's yard, she took out her bit of blanket and folded it into a thick pad. Then she reached up and settled it on top of the broken glass. In a couple of seconds, she was up and over, tugging the blanket after her.

If she made a sound, she was dead meat. The Cavalieris lived over the chippie and next door were Geoffrey and Fat Annie. She had to be totally, absolutely silent. Tightening the straps of her rucksack, she dried her hands on her leggings. Then she began to pull herself up the drainpipe.

It was like being in a dark, private world, locked into her own concentration. Up the drainpipe on to the extension. Along the extension to the main building. Up on to the windowsill . . .

The drainpipe was fine, just as she'd expected, but when she put her foot on to the windowsill she felt the edge crack. The wood was old and crumbling, and she had to lean sideways and run her fingers over it to find a safe part.

Trusting her weight to the right hand edge of the sill, she reached up for the gutter. Thinking, *It's got to be OK.* Everything depended on that and its brackets.

The first bracket she tried felt risky, but the second was as solid as a rock. Putting one foot on the lintel at the top of the window, she pulled herself up and planted the other on the bracket. Then she was up, leaning into the slope of the roof, crawling over the tiles and up towards the ridge.

She heard a burst of sound from the other side of the building as two cars roared down the Row together. *Joyriders*, she thought. With any luck, they would circle round behind the Newenthal flats and come back down the Row a second time.

She waited for them. As the scream of brakes and

the noise of their engines filled the Row again, she crawled on to the ridge, letting them camouflage the faint sounds she made.

Then they went for good, racing off towards the industrial estate, and she was on her own. Exposed. Anyone who looked up could see her. Drunks out late. People from the flats opposite. Police cars patrolling the Row. From the moment her head came over the top, she was in the front line.

Gathering her feet under her, she stood up, and saw the Row spread out below her. On the side she'd come from, there was a web of old, terraced streets. She could pick out her own house by the street light outside Mrs Macdonald's.

Opposite, facing her across the Row, were the five huge blocks of the Newenthal flats. Toronto House and Canberra House. Marshall and Livingstone and Nightingale. They dwarfed the cinema and the single storey shops in front of them.

For a second, she stood looking down at it all. The place where she lived, spread out for her to see. Then her concentration sharpened and she focused on the wall. Steadily she walked along the ridge towards it.

It looked ten times as big as it did from ground level. She ran her hands over the rough, dirty surface and slid her rucksack round to the front, so that she could reach the spray-cans without taking it off.

She knew exactly what she was going to do. No fancy pictures. Those were fine in the right place—she had a brilliant Mickey Mouse on the side of Nightingale House—but this was the sort of wall where you had to write your tag or nothing. And she was going to do it full size in four colours. With shadows, to show she'd taken her time.

She pulled out the black can and stood there, feeling the adrenalin come. It would only take one wrong line to blow the whole thing—but she wasn't going to blow it.

Her finger pushed down on the button.

She laid out the letters as if she were dancing. Five lovely shapes, in a level straight line, all exactly the same size. Perfectly spaced to fill the whole width of the wall. When she reached the end, she went back and doubled up the black on the shadow side, to make the whole thing solid.

That would have done, of course. She'd written enough to amaze people. But she wanted something better this time, and she glanced up and down the Row, to check it was still empty, and then swapped the black can for the yellow.

Yellow at the top of every letter, shading down through orange to red. That was how she'd planned it.

The paint went on like a dream. She couldn't see the real colours in the faint, false light of the street

20

lamps, but she could sense the weight of them. Airy yellow at the top, gathering down through orange, to the heavy, heavy red. It felt so good that she let the red spill out at the bottom in drops of blood, one under each letter. Big, swelling drops, with a highlight on each one.

If she outlined those drops in black, it would be the best tag she'd ever seen. She dropped the red can into the rucksack and felt for the black, grinning like an idiot.

Then she heard the joyriders coming back. She glanced sideways—and saw a movement in the shadows across the road.

There was a figure standing on the pathway at the side of the cinema. She couldn't make out much, but she could see a face turned towards the roof of the chippie.

Someone was down there, watching her.

Don't panic, she thought. *Keep calm.* She dropped the can back into her rucksack and started to move back along the ridge, keeping half an eye on the watcher.

The figure was still motionless by the time she slid down the roof and lost sight of it. For a moment she wondered whether she would be safer hiding in the yard, but she didn't fancy being trapped. Better to get home, if she could.

As she let herself down on to the windowsill, feeling

for a secure foothold, she was listening all the time. Trying to catch the sound of a footstep among the other night noises. Twice, she was convinced that she heard a sound in the service road, but when she reached the ground everything was silent outside the yard.

She threw up her blanket pad and heaved herself on to the wall. There was no one in sight. The watcher—whoever it was—hadn't come round to catch her.

She jumped down, pulled the blanket after her and crept out into the street. No one there, either.

She didn't see anyone, all the way home. Even the old drunk in the alley had disappeared. As she slid through the fence, she was feeling triumphant.

I managed it! I tagged that wall without getting caught!

She went through the back door, pulled it shut after her and locked it. With a click.

It was the first careless thing she'd done. For a second she froze, waiting for her mother to shout. But there was nothing. No sound.

She was safe. And she'd done it. Grinning in the dark, she crept up the stairs to her bed.

PAULINE
Does she think I'm unconscious? Or deaf? Does she really think I can't hear the door?

I've tried talking to her, but she just gives me that

blank, blue-eyed stare. Why would I go out at three in the morning? Honestly, Mum! You must have dreamt it. *She won't admit anything.*

If I felt better, I'd try and catch her, but at the moment—it's hopeless. By the time I've struggled out of bed, she's away. I tried sitting up once, right by the door, but she didn't go out that night. And next day I could hardly move.

It's not every night, you see. And never two nights in a row. She'll go weeks and weeks—months, even— without stirring out of bed. And then, when I think it's all over, I'll hear that little creak at the top of the stairs that always wakes me up. And I'll lie there sweating. No, God, please God. Don't let it be that. Let me be imagining it.

Sometimes He answers me, and there's no more sound, so I know the stair must have creaked on its own. But sometimes the second creak comes, halfway down, and then I know it's real. It's no use calling out, because she won't answer. I just lie there with my fists screwed up and the prayer going on and on in my head. Don't let her go out. Please, God, don't let her go out. *And then—after I've heard the door click—* Don't let anything happen to her. Please, God, don't let anything happen. Keep her safe out there.

She doesn't understand. I've tried talking to her, and telling her about the gangs and the drugs and the joyriding. She knows that terrible things happen round here, like that fight when Tony Cavalieri was crippled. But she thinks she can handle anything.

You can't blame her, I suppose. She does handle a lot of things at the moment. Helping me out. She cooks and cleans and shops. And does the washing. And she manages all right at school. And she's not anorexic and she's not on drugs and she doesn't go out with boys . . .

I lie there in the dark, telling myself all those things. Telling them over like beads in a rosary. She's strong and sensible and she's never got into trouble so far . . .

But none of it's any use. It would only take one drunk. One junkie. One man with a knife. Whatever she's doing, she can't be safe out there in the street. In the dark. On her own.

And suppose she's not on her own . . . ?

Sometimes I think I ought to tell Janet. But she'd make such a fuss. She might even try and take Ashley to live with her, like Karen and Louise. And it's not as if—

It's only till I'm feeling better. Then I'll sort everything out. And Ashley won't have to work so hard then. It's just that I need a bit of help at the moment . . .

3

The next morning, Vikki was there on the doorstep at half-past eight.

Ashley was still making her mother's lunchtime sandwich, chewing a piece of bread while she did it. When the door bell rang, she guessed who it was and she darted down the hall.

'You're OK!' Vikki said, before the door was properly open.

Ashley put a hand over her mouth and nodded towards the front room. 'Sssh!'

Vikki jerked her head free. 'I couldn't sleep a wink!' She'd dropped her voice, but her whisper was just as dramatic. 'I felt sick all night!'

'Must have been some party,' Ashley said.

'I hardly *noticed* the party! Honestly, Ash, I couldn't dance, or . . . or do anything. I just kept worrying about you. Matt thought I was being silly, and we had the most terrible row—'

'You didn't tell him?' Ashley said quickly.

'Of course not!' But Vikki's eyes flickered, and she looked away.

Ashley wondered whether to push it. Then she let it go. It was too late now, anyway.

'Well, everything's OK,' she said. 'Look at me. I'm all in one piece.'

'That's good. Because I need you to talk to Matt when we get to school. He's really annoyed with me. D'you think you can—?'

'I suppose so.' Just then, Ashley was more interested in the tag. 'Have you seen the wall? What d'you think?'

Vikki's eyes opened wide. 'It's absolutely—'

That was as far as she got, because Pauline called from the front room. 'Ashie? Who's that? You'll be late for school if you don't hurry.'

'You mustn't be late!' Vikki hissed. 'If you get lunchtime detention, you won't be able to talk to Matt—'

'OK, OK.' Ashley looked at her watch. 'Why don't you go on ahead?' She had no chance of getting through everything with Vikki hanging around. 'I'll catch you up.'

Vikki nodded and whirled away, and Ashley looked into the front room. 'Sorry, Mum. That was Vikki. I'll just get your breakfast and then I'll come and help you get dressed.'

Pauline heaved herself up on one elbow. 'Don't be silly. You haven't got time.'

'I can't just leave you. I haven't even brushed your hair.'

26

'I'll probably be able to manage myself. In a bit. You go to school.'

'But—' Ashley knew she ought to insist, but she could see the clock over her mother's shoulder. She let herself pretend. 'Well, if you're sure. I'll just get your breakfast.'

She ran into the kitchen and tipped some cereal into a bowl. Then she added milk and poured out a glass of orange juice.

'Is that enough?' she said, as she carried them into the front room.

'Of course.' Pauline struggled up in bed and leaned forward to let Ashley put a pillow behind her back. 'You get off to school!'

Ashley kissed her on the nose and snatched up her school bag. 'Be good, then. See you later!'

She raced up the road at top speed. It wasn't just to avoid being late. She was dying to see her wall.

When she reached the end of the road and swung round the corner, it shouted down at her. Yellow like the sun. Screeching orange. Red as a pillarbox. The best thing she'd ever done. CINDY.

It sang in her head all day, and she found herself grinning at people and humming under her breath. None of them knew who Cindy was—no one knew except Vikki—but when they saw the tag they would envy her. Because she'd dared to climb up there.

All day, she looked forward to the end of the afternoon. To walking back with Vikki and seeing the wall again.

But when that moment came, it was like a slap round the face.

She and Vikki walked through the Newenthal flats and up the side of the cinema, to come out by the traffic lights on the Row. Facing the wall.

And the wall was bright white. All over.

Fat Annie must have phoned a painter the moment she saw the tag. It hadn't even lasted twenty-four hours. *The mean, miserable . . .*

'The cow,' Vikki said.

Ashley was too stunned to reply. She didn't even notice when the lights changed. She was left behind, staring up at the white paint while everyone else surged across the road. By the time Vikki noticed, and started yelling at her from the other side of the road, it was too late to move. The cars had surged forward and she was cut off. Looking at a blank wall.

She hadn't left any mark on it. She was nothing.

'Makes you sick, doesn't it?' said a voice from beside her.

She jumped and looked round.

There was a boy leaning against the traffic lights, lounging back with one long leg crossed over the other. He was chewing gum, working it round and round in his mouth.

He nodded across the road, towards the wall. 'It was a great bit of writing. A real gob in the eye for Annie.'

It sounded funny the way he said it. *A real gob in the eye*. As if he was using someone else's voice. Ashley looked cautiously at him. He was older than she was, a thin, gangling boy with big hands and feet and a white, bony face, like a clown's. Wisps of curly hair poked out from under his old striped bobble hat.

'You don't want to fall out with Annie,' he said. 'If you touch her property, she stamps on your fingers.'

'Maybe someone ought to stamp back.' Ashley was still feeling sore and disappointed.

The boy shifted his chewing gum to the other cheek. 'Great idea. How are you going to do it?'

Ashley felt herself go cold. Cold and very still inside. 'Do what?' she said.

He didn't answer. He just looked up at the white wall and then back at her face.

He knew.

'Do what?' Ashley said again, trying to sound bewildered.

The boy pulled a long string of chewing gum out

of his mouth. 'OK. *If* you'd done that,' he nodded towards the wall, 'how would you get back at her for painting it over?'

'I'd tag the wall again,' Ashley said. '*If* it was me.'

The boy's mouth stopped moving and he looked her straight in the eyes. The lights changed above his head and the people round them began to cross the road, but he ignored that. He was staring at Ashley, and the stare kept her there too.

'You're going up again tonight?' he murmured.

Oh no, you don't. 'That's what I would do,' Ashley said tartly. '*If* it was me.'

She could have saved her breath. 'You want to watch out,' the boy said solemnly. 'Annie's going to have Geoffrey on guard.' He pushed his face forward suddenly and barked at her. 'You get out there, Geoffrey! Get out and watch. Don't you let those kids at my wall!'

It was Annie. Annie to the life. His whole body even seemed to thicken. Ashley choked on a giggle.

But while she was still giggling, the boy's face changed. He was someone else now. He lowered his eyes shiftily, peering under the lids, and his tongue moved over his lips. Flick, flick.

'Maybe . . . um . . . it's a girl,' he muttered. 'I . . . I might catch . . . um . . . a girl . . . ' And his hand snaked out, heading for Ashley's arm.

For a moment it *was* the Hyena's hand, reaching out for her, and she jumped back, feeling clammy and revolted.

The boy's tongue flicked over his lips again. 'Maybe . . . um . . . you're not so tough?'

'I'm fine,' Ashley said defiantly. She spotted a gap in the cars and launched herself over the road, without waiting for the lights to change.

But the boy was right behind. As she hit the opposite pavement, he drew level, whispering in her ear.

'Pity about those drops of blood.'

'Don't know what you mean,' Ashley muttered.

He laughed at her, under his breath. 'You should have gone round them. In black.'

That was it! She could take all the other stuff, but art criticism was the last straw. Ashley stopped dead and scowled at him.

'OK!' she snapped. 'Take a look tomorrow then! And see if you could do better!'

His face was transformed. As if that was what he'd been waiting for, he gave her a grin and vanished into the crowd. Ashley tried to see where he went, but there was no chance to watch, because Vikki was there, at her elbow, hissing eagerly into her ear.

'Why was he talking to you? What did he say?'

'What? Who?' Ashley blinked and turned round. 'What was who talking about?'

'That boy,' Vikki frowned. 'Honestly, Ash, don't you know who he is?'

Ashley couldn't see what all the fuss was about. 'Just some boy.'

'Don't be daft. Haven't you seen him? He goes round with *Eddie Beale.*'

It still wasn't making sense. 'Who's Eddie Beale?'

The moment the words were out, Ashley knew she'd said something stupid. Vikki's eyes opened wide and she gave a squeal. 'You're kidding! Come on, Ash, you *are* kidding?'

Ashley shook her head. 'I've never heard of Eddie Beale.'

VIKKI

I couldn't believe it. Who's Eddie Beale? she said, and I could see she wasn't joking. I didn't think you could live on the Row, or anywhere near it, and not know about Eddie.

But then, this is Ashley we're talking about. Every mother's dream daughter. I've never heard her swear. Never seen her smoke. She doesn't stay out late or hang around in the street—except when she's doing that crazy writing—and she never, never, never gets into trouble at school. She hasn't even had her ears pierced.

Don't get me wrong. She's my best friend, and I

always go to her when I'm in trouble, because she can keep secrets and she's really sensible. She doesn't just nod and agree with you, either. When I had that row with Matt, and he cut my purple jacket to bits, she really let me have it.

'It's all your own fault. You shouldn't have stood him up.'

'It was only a joke—'

'Some joke. You should have guessed the other kids would laugh at him. And you know what his temper's like.'

She was certainly right about that. He's got a real red-head's temper. Like all his family. You should see him and his sister Ginger when they get going.

Ash grabbed my arm and marched me across the playground, then and there, and made me apologize to Matt. Then she went off and left us alone. That's another good thing about her. She doesn't try to own you. She's great about people.

But she doesn't know about . . . things. Outside school, she's like a baby. Doesn't know who the dealers are, or where the party's going to be, or who's out to get who. She's straight home and into that house and you don't see her again until school the next day.

I thought I was used to all that. I wasn't even surprised she didn't recognize that kid at the traffic lights. But then she comes out with it.

Who's Eddie Beale? *And I'm, like—where do I start?*

Hasn't she seen Eddie walking up the Row, as if he owned the place? With Dougie Barrett and Shaun James behind him acting really heavy. Hasn't she even looked through her window and seen the flash cars go past, with all the kids cheering and waving? Eddie wired a BMW last week and drove it right past the police station, cool as a cucumber.

People are always talking about him. Last winter, he suddenly turned up on Mrs Barrett's doorstep, when they were going to cut her electricity off. He said, 'There you are, Ma. Present from me and Doug.' But from the way Doug went round singing his praises, you could see he didn't know anything about it beforehand. Eddie's like that. If he fancies doing something, he just does it.

I tell you, if that boy had spoken to me at the traffic lights, I'd have been so-o-o-o cool and funny, to try and get him to tell Eddie about me. I'd want him to say, 'I saw this really amazing girl yesterday.' So Eddie would fancy meeting me.

That would be brilliant, wouldn't it? Just imagine. Eddie Beale hears about me, and he comes down the Row at ten to four, just to catch me on the way home from school. He wouldn't be looking out, of course. That's not his style. He'd be on the corner, with that kid and two or three friends. Shaun and Doug and Phil Carson maybe.

So I come across at the lights and all the other girls are, like—WOW! That's EDDIE BEALE! *And they're all eyeing him up and talking extra loud to each other, to get him to notice them.*

But I'm being really cool, just chatting to Ashley— no, maybe Ashley's had to go home early. Maybe I'm on my own and looking really great and a bit dreamy. With this little smile—like that—as if I'm standing back and watching the others acting like idiots. And I don't even notice Eddie because I'm so busy thinking about Matt ...

No, I think I'm deciding to give Matt up. For his own good, of course, because he's so dependent on me. That means I'm really sad, and I don't even notice Eddie. I'm going right by him when he sticks his hand out and touches my arm and it's, like ... like fire.

The moment he touches me, I just know that this is it. So he's ten years older than me. Who cares about that? I look round real slow, waiting for the wisecrack, and there's complete silence because for a moment—just for a moment—he actually can't speak because he's felt it too, and ... and we're in this bubble together ... and everything's very slow ... and we're staring at each other ... and then he says ...

Eddie Beale says ...

He says to me ...

Oh, wouldn't it be great?

4

When Vikki had got over being amazed, she tried to explain about Eddie Beale, but Ashley hardly listened. Who cared about some man with a gang? She'd got much more important problems than that.

What had got into her at the traffic lights? She'd given herself away to that boy in the bobble hat. *Take a look tomorrow!* she'd said. What had possessed her? Now he knew for sure that she was Cindy.

She'd only been boasting, anyway. She couldn't really go out again tonight, not with the Hyena watching out for her. It would be crazy.

Maybe that was a good thing. The boy would come past tomorrow and see a wall that was still blank. Maybe he'd decide that he'd picked on the wrong person after all.

Ashley tried to look on the bright side, but it didn't help much. She said goodbye to Vikki and trailed home, feeling sour and sick. By the time she reached home, she was at rock bottom—or so she thought.

But when she slid her key into the lock, there was a voice from the kitchen.

'There she is, Pauline! I'll put the kettle on.'

Suddenly, everything was ten times as bad. Janet was there.

Ashley had no time to gather her wits. The moment she opened the door, the twins came bouncing out of the front room.

'Look, Ashley, we've got our hair different! Don't you think mine's great?' Karen grabbed her hand and swung on it, gabbling at top speed.

Louise didn't say a word, but she threw herself at Ashley's other side, like a chimpanzee, hugging her round the waist.

'Hi,' Ashley said.

Janet's head came poking round the front room door. 'Surprise, surprise! It's your horrible aunt and your beastly little sisters!'

That was supposed to be a joke, but it was clumsy and lumbering, like everything about Janet, and it was too near the truth. Ashley smiled politely and pretended that she was glad to see them.

'Hi,' she said again.

Karen was giggling and dragging her into the room, but Louise let go suddenly and stepped back, plaiting her fingers together. She picked up a lot more than Karen did. Ashley felt like a rat. She smiled and put a hand on Louise's head.

'It's nice to see you, Lou.'

She was only seven. She couldn't help what Janet was like.

They couldn't have been there very long, but the whole house reeked of Janet, already. Furniture polish and hot ironing. Ashley was barely through the door before Janet's arm slid round her shoulders.

'How are you, darling? Tired?'

'I'm fine,' Ashley said. Meaning, *No, I'm not tired. I can cope. All right?* She went across the room to kiss her mother. 'Hallo. Did you have a good day?'

Her mother's eyes flickered at her, sending unspoken messages. Ashley could read them horribly well. Pauline was out of bed, sitting in a chair and dressed in clothes she would never have chosen herself. Janet had picked out a thick jumper and trousers. She'd brushed Pauline's hair until it gleamed as well—and Ashley knew how long that took—and tied it back with a ribbon.

Ashley could imagine the whole scene. The key in the front door. Janet's head peering round. *Hallo, Pauline! I've brought the girls to see you!* And then the frown, as she saw her sister's nightdress. *Why don't you two girls go and play in the garden while I sort things out a bit?*

Janet's arm tightened, pulling Ashley towards the kitchen. 'Let's go and have a cup of tea, shall we? Give the girls a bit of time alone with their mum.'

She shut the door behind them and patted a stool, as if it were her own home and Ashley was the visitor. 'Sit down and have a rest.'

'I'm fine,' Ashley said again.

Janet didn't answer straight away. She just smiled and made a complicated business out of pouring the hot water into the teapot and finding the cups. But when the tea was poured, she sat down next to Ashley and patted her hand.

'Look, you don't have to pretend. It might do you good to have a moan.'

Prod, prod, prod. Ashley felt like a mouse in a hole, with a sharp stick poking at her. She edged away and picked up her teacup.

'I'm fine. Everything's fine.'

Janet sighed. 'You're managing really well, darling, but—things aren't really fine, are they? Pauline's getting worse. Don't you think we ought to try and find you some help?'

Ashley's fingers tightened round the cup. 'I can manage. Mum's just going through a bit of a bad patch.'

'You wouldn't like to come and stay with us for a bit? For a rest?'

'No,' Ashley said. It was too fast to be polite. She said it again, more carefully. 'No thank you. We like it here.'

Janet sighed again and bit her lip. *Any minute now,* Ashley thought, *she's going to put her arm round my shoulders again.*

She did.

'I know what Pauline's like,' she said. 'She's a fighter. But it's your life too. If we got on to the doctor and the Social Services—'

'That's ridiculous! She just needs a bit of help at the moment, that's all. And I can cope.'

Janet's arm fell away. This time her voice was colder. 'So that's why she was sitting round in bed in her nightdress? At half-past three?'

'She's not usually in her nightdress,' Ashley said stubbornly. 'I was a bit late today, that's all.'

'Just today?' Janet raised her eyebrows.

'Yes!'

'You really are loyal, aren't you?' Janet's fat, ringed hand patted Ashley's shoulder.

Ashley resisted the longing to twist her head sideways and bite it.

From the front room, she could hear the sound of the twins' voices, getting more and more excited. Karen kept giving whoops of wild laughter, and even Louise was giggling. Janet nodded towards the door.

'They need their mother, you see. If she came to live with us, they could be like that all the time.'

That's all you know, Ashley thought sourly. Pauline

40

always put on a good show for the twins, but by the time they went she would be exhausted. She'd probably cry before she went to bed, and it would take her hours to relax enough to fall asleep.

But once she is asleep, she'll be out for hours . . .

The thought came by itself. Ashley really hadn't meant to think about the wall again, but suddenly, with the picture of her mother fast asleep, she saw herself moving through the night. Sliding out into the darkness with her spray-cans.

Who would know if she did go? No one. Not if she didn't get caught. Surely she could outwit the Hyena?

The idea danced in her head. Suddenly, she found herself smiling at Janet. *You'd faint if you knew what's in my mind. You'd die.* She reached for the big cake tin and took the lid off.

'Have some chocolate cake,' she said.

It was all right now. She was on top again, and Janet couldn't touch her. No one could touch her.

LOUISE

Janet's always strange after we've been to see Mum. She keeps asking us questions. Mummy was looking all right today, wasn't she? And Ashley looked very happy, didn't she? *The sort of questions that make you say the answer she wants.*

Mummy was fine. She laughed all the time. But Janet wasn't happy. Going to see Mum always makes her miserable. I could feel it all the way home. I wanted to snuggle up to her on the bus, so she could hug me, but Karen sat in the middle and I couldn't get near.

Karen kept on and on talking. 'Ashley's road isn't as nice as ours, is it, Janet? Why haven't the houses got front gardens? Gardens are much nicer. Why don't Mummy and Ashley live in our road? Why don't they come and live with us?'

She's so silly. Anyone can see that Frank wouldn't like it. He likes pretending that we're his little girls. So does Janet. That's why they've got all those photos in the lounge, looking like Mummy and Daddy with their children. It fits really nicely.

As long as you don't think about Mummy and Ashley, living in that dirty place.

There's such a lot of broken things there. Cars with all the wheels missing. Houses with wood over the windows. Big, coloured scribbles on the walls. Tiger. Super-Cindy. *Silly words that don't make sense.*

Mummy said, 'Why don't you stay a bit longer? Ashley can go out and get some pizzas.' But Janet said we had to get back before it was dark. She never says that when we go to see Frank's family. We always walk home late, and she tells us the stars.

Perhaps they don't have stars here.

I think I'd be scared here, in the dark. There's some places that feel horrible, like that alley behind the shops. And the chip shop, where the fat man looks through the upstairs window.

I'm glad I don't have to live here.

5

After Janet took the twins away, the house was quiet and empty. Ashley spread her homework out on the table in the front room and tried to cheer Pauline up by asking her questions about History and French. Sometimes it worked, but that night neither of them was interested.

Pauline lay back in the lumpy, uncomfortable chair and shook her head. 'I'm sorry, but I can't. I just can't. I think I'll go to bed after tea.'

'You can go now if you like.'

Pauline shook her head again. 'Not before tea.'

Why not? Ashley was going to say. But she bit her tongue. She knew the answer. Only invalids had their meals in bed.

She took out her books and tried to start on her homework, but it was impossible to concentrate. Every time she looked up, she saw Pauline's grey, exhausted face. After twenty minutes, she hadn't written a word, and she knew she wasn't going to. Standing up, she swept the books into her bag.

'What do you want for tea?'

Pauline closed her eyes. 'I think—Ashie, I'm really not very hungry. Maybe I'll go to bed now.'

'Do you want me to bring you some scrambled egg when you're lying down?'

'I said I'm not hungry!'

Pauline's voice was sharp. It was a waste of time to argue. Ashley helped her wash and change into her nightdress, and then she left her to go to sleep.

The house was even quieter then. Ashley found she didn't want more than scrambled egg herself. She ate it in the kitchen and went upstairs without giving her homework another thought. She was just waiting until it was late enough to go out.

When she did, it was quiet outside, as well. There was no one sleeping in Mrs Macdonald's alley. There were no joyriders up on the Row. The whole place was eerily still, and Ashley went up the road in something like a trance, sliding from shadow to shadow.

When she reached the entrance of the service road, she stopped for ten minutes, standing motionless and listening. There was nothing. No sound. No sign of anyone about. She padded along to the yard behind the chippie and threw her blanket over the broken glass at the top of the wall.

Even the flap of the blanket seemed loud in the stillness. Every second of the way up to the roof, she was tense and nervous, expecting someone—Fat

45

Annie or the Hyena—to come charging out of the shop next door, yelling about the police.

There was nothing.

Like someone in a dream, she padded along the rooftop to her wall. It was twice as beautiful now that it was painted white. A perfect surface, waiting to show up her tag. This time, it was going to look stupendous.

She focused on that, forgetting everything else. Pulling out the black spray-can, she swung her arm down in a great semi-circle, making the shape of the first letter.

And then the second.

And then the third . . .

The whole thing was almost finished, and she was just shading the last drop of blood, when she heard the sound of the gate opening, down in the chip shop yard. A faint, rusty scrape. Her head jerked round abruptly, and she saw a shifting shadow slide in through the gate.

Someone was standing in the yard, waiting for her to come down.

If she hadn't heard, she would have walked straight into the trap. And then—A split-second horror movie played itself out in her head. She saw herself finishing off that last drop of blood, sliding down triumphantly off the roof, and—GOTCHA!

She would have slithered straight into the Hyena's arms. She imagined him hanging on to her legs and yelling for the police. And all the social workers and Auntie Janets in the world racing up to wag their fingers at her.

Bad girl! You're out of control! You can't cope!

Well, they were out of luck. She'd spotted him down there and she was going to work out a way to escape. Even though she was twenty feet above ground with no way down but the drainpipe.

But first she was going to finish her tag. Her hand tightened round the spray-can and she finished that last drop of blood, filling the black outline with crimson, except for the little highlight. Then she put the can away and slipped her rucksack round, on to her back. So. Now she needed a plan.

And that was when the Row erupted.

Half a dozen cars roared round the corner and squealed to a stop outside Fat Annie's, screeching their brakes and burning rubber. People jumped out and started banging on Annie's front door, yelling and swearing and kicking at the paintwork.

Ashley froze, trying to work out what to do. The gang down there sounded crazy enough to take the whole house to bits. If Annie phoned the police, they might not stop at the gang. They might look up on the roof as well. And then—

At the back of the shop, a window rattled down. Annie's voice bellowed into the night.

'Geoffrey! Don't bother about the roof. Go and stop that lot! You hear me?'

Ashley couldn't believe her ears. The Hyena had trouble tackling Vikki about a copy of *Penthouse*. What was he supposed to do with a gang of twenty rowdies? He'd be petrified.

Petrified or not, he didn't hesitate. Ashley saw his dark shape move again, pushing the yard gate open. A moment later, he appeared at the end of the alley, caught in the glow of the street lamp. He edged round the corner of the buildings, towards the Row.

For a minute, Ashley couldn't believe he was so stupid. Then she came to her senses and seized the chance he'd given her. Running along the ridge, she slithered down to the guttering. By now, she knew the footholds exactly, and in a couple of seconds she was on the extension roof. There was no need to be careful. The noise at the front of the shop masked any sounds she made.

She slid down the drainpipe so fast that she scorched her hands. When her feet hit the ground, they were already running, and she crossed the yard in three strides. There was no need to climb the wall, because the Hyena had left the gate open. She raced through it at top speed.

And someone grabbed her arm, holding on tightly. No!

No, no *no*! It wasn't fair!

She flung herself sideways, trying to break free, but whoever was holding her was very strong. His hands clamped her arm so hard that she wanted to scream. She actually opened her mouth—

'Don't blow it,' whispered someone on the other side of her.

Slowly her mouth closed. She recognized the voice. And now she could see the shape of his silly bobble hat, outlined against the light at the end of the service road. It was Eddie Beale's boy.

'She's OK now, Doug,' he said. 'Let's go.'

The hands gripping Ashley's arm loosened suddenly, and the boy caught hold of her hand.

'Hurry up. Before the Hyena gets back.'

He shot off, pulling Ashley after him. Doug raced on ahead. By the time they came out into Railway Street, he was already twenty metres down it, heading away from the Row.

He stopped beside a parked car and hauled the door open. The boy sprinted towards it, still dragging Ashley, and pushed her into the back, ahead of him.

She tried to struggle against him, but he hissed in her ear. 'Don't be stupid. You'll never make it home without the Hyena seeing you. Get down on the floor!'

Ashley gave in and slid into the car with him, and Doug piled in after them, crouching low as well. 'Let's get going, Joe,' he grunted.

'Not yet.' The boy was kneeling on the seat with his head down, peering through the back window. 'He's not in sight yet.'

Ashley was wedged on to the floor, with no idea what was happening. She started to feel the door next to her, hunting for the handle, but before she found it the boy hissed triumphantly.

'Yes! They're on their way. Sock it to them, Sam!'

Ashley had thought there were only three of them in the car, but suddenly someone shot up in the front seat, reaching for the controls. The engine started with a cough and they screamed away from the kerb, with a jerk that flung Ashley back against the seat.

The boy was bouncing up and down like a maniac. 'Look at them, Doug! They're going crazy! They're *demented*.'

He went into a frenzied version of his Hyena voice, stuttering and stammering so much that he almost choked.

'I . . . um . . . you can't . . . but that's our—'

A woman's voice yelled from the driving seat. 'Sit down, Joe, or you'll go through the windscreen.'

He slithered down into a sitting position, just as she flung the car round a corner, and he and Doug started to laugh helplessly, throwing themselves around. Ashley hauled herself off the floor and squeezed on to the seat.

'What's going on?' she said. 'What's so funny?'

The car lurched the other way, round another corner, and Joe fell against her, gasping for breath.

'The car . . . it's . . . it's . . .

He couldn't get the words out. It was Doug who told her.

'We've got the Hyena's car. And he and Annie are going loony.'

SAM

Yes! Oh, yesss! I've really got to her this time!

That's one of our games, Eddie's and mine. Getting to Annie. She pretends to ignore us most of the time. Won't even speak to us if we go into the shop. Looks down her nose at us, as if we were rubbish.

No one treats me like rubbish.

So we get our own back. It's not always like this, though. Usually, it's more . . . subtle.

Like last week. I caught the Hyena outside, straightening that vegetable stand they have in front of the shop and I went right up to him. Really close, so we were almost touching.

'Hi there,' I said. 'What's the matter? Someone been playing with your apples?'

51

And I reached across (just being helpful) and moved one of the apples to a better position, brushing my arm against his chest. Accidentally, of course. Then I fluttered my eyelashes at him and he went pink. Stammered so hard he couldn't get the words out.

'Th-thank you, b-b-but . . . '

I could see Eddie out of the corner of my eye. He was watching us with that twisty smile of his, and I knew I'd amused him. That was good enough for me, really, but just then Annie came lumbering out of the shop. Like a rhino rushing to protect its cub. And I thought, Aha!

She looked down her nose at me with her you are garbage expression. `That will do, thank you very much. We don't need any help from people like you.'

And she reached across and tugged at my arm, to get me out of range of the Hyena.

Oh, fantastic! Another five points at least. But I couldn't leave it like that. I could feel Eddie watching to see how far I'd go. If I could come out on top now she'd started pushing me around.

No problem. I didn't even need to think. I just went where she pushed me, until she started pulling the Hyena back into the shop. Then I called. Very suddenly, so they wouldn't be able to stop themselves reacting.

'Hey!'

Their heads snapped round, and I gave the Hyena a long, long stare—you know the kind of stare—and ran my tongue over my top lip. He went beetroot. It was the funniest thing I've ever seen in my life. He was sweating with embarrassment.

Annie grabbed his shoulder and shouted, 'Tart!' at me. Then she threw him into the shop in front of her. But it was too late by then. There must have been fifty people in the Row and they were all in fits.

Eddie held out his arm to me, as if I was coming off a stage, and then paraded me right down to Shepherds Corner. And people were cheering all the way.

Eddie and me, we understand each other. We knew it the moment we met. I've got to have a strong man, that I don't need to make excuses for, and Eddie is the strong man. The King. Walking down the Row with him is like being in a procession. Everyone's watching, and he always gives them a show for their money.

There's nobody like him.

We're equals, and we respect each other.

6

Ashley sat bolt upright. 'You mean—we've stolen this car?'

That just made it worse. It sent Joe hysterical, and Sam started falling about too. She shrieked with laughter, flinging herself from side to side in the seat as she drove.

Doug leaned over from the back and thumped her shoulder. 'Knock it off. You want to mince us all?' He tried to hold her steady, but that only made her laugh even more. She shrieked like a lunatic and the car swerved right across the road.

Joe stopped laughing too, and banged on the back of the seat. 'You're out of your tree, Sam. Calm down. We've got to ditch the car. Annie's bound to have the police on our tails. Pull in by those garages.'

Whatever Sam was on, it was happy stuff. She didn't argue. Humming loudly, she spun the wheel, throwing Ashley against Joe, and they roared across the tarmac in front of the garages. She jammed on the brakes and it looked as if they were going to stop just in time, before they hit the far wall.

But, just at the last moment, she swung the wheel and sent the car crashing into the nearest garage.

There was a loud clank, and a crunch, and then the engine died.

'You *maniac*!' Joe said. 'Let's get out of here!'

They hadn't travelled very far. They were round the other side of the Newenthal flats, close to the school. Joe slithered out and reached back to pull Ashley after him.

'Quick!' he said.

Ashley dithered, untangling her rucksack from the seatbelts, and he tugged at her arm.

'What are you doing? Waiting for the police? *Out!*'

Doug was pushing her from behind, and Sam was out already, running past the garages, towards the flats, and the three of them raced after her.

Ashley could see that she knew the estate. A stranger would have stayed on the main paths, between the tower blocks, but Sam struck out across the grass, doubling unpredictably round corners. Two or three times they would have lost her, except for the fluttering end of the long scarf she was wearing.

By the time she ran out of breath, she was round the back of Toronto House, in the dark patch where the winos hid out. There was no one there that night except Spider Mo, tucked up snoring among her carrier bags. Sam stopped next to her, leaned against the wall and slid slowly down it. When the others caught up, she was sitting on the ground with her legs out straight in front of her.

'You sad cow,' Doug said. 'What were you doing? Trying to kill us all?'

Sam looked up at him and smiled, as if he'd paid her a compliment. Even sitting on the ground, completely out of it, she was shining. She had the kind of face you see on magazine covers. Maybe not more beautiful than everyone else—she had jagged blonde hair and gaps between her teeth—but twice as real.

Doug caught hold of her hands and hauled her up. 'Time you were home,' he said. 'It's been a long night.'

Sam nodded sleepily. 'Cold,' she said. Bending over, she unwrapped her long scarf and wound it solemnly round Spider Mo's shoulders. Mo stirred for a moment, growling in her sleep. Then she settled back into the middle of her bags.

Doug pulled at Sam's arm. 'Let's go,' he said firmly.

The two of them turned and began to walk away.

'Hey—' Ashley took a step after them, but Joe caught at her arm, holding her back.

'What's the matter?'

'They're just leaving us here. And it's the middle of the night.'

'So?' Joe looked scornful. 'Who's going to touch us? Everyone knows Eddie looks after me.'

Spider Mo stirred at their feet. She wasn't awake, but her long arms were groping around, feeling for her belongings. Joe stepped back as one of her hands brushed his ankle.

'Let's go. She'll make a racket if she wakes up. I'll walk along with you if you like.'

Ashley fell into step beside him as they headed for the Row, going up to Shepherds Corner to avoid passing Fat Annie's.

'You'll be safe on your own soon,' Joe said cheerfully. 'When people see you hanging round with Eddie, they'll lay off you.'

'What are you talking about?' Ashley said. She hadn't hung around with anyone since she was seven. 'I've never even met Eddie Beale.'

Joe grinned. 'You will. Now he's taking an interest in you.'

'How can he be taking an interest in me? He's never even heard of me.'

'Oh, come *on*. You think we were there by accident tonight?'

Ashley hadn't thought about it. Things had been moving too fast for her to work out what was going on. Now she started to work it out.

'You mean—you were there on purpose? To help me out?'

Joe nodded, still grinning. 'I told Eddie you were

going to paint that wall again. And he said, "She'll need a bit of back-up then. Annie won't get caught twice. Maybe you ought to hang around with a few of the others." We were watching out for you for hours before you turned up, but he was right, wasn't he?'

'But why would he bother? He doesn't know me at all.'

'I bet he knows about you. There aren't many things he misses round here. And he's . . . ' Joe hesitated and looked sideways at Ashley. 'You'll be OK. Like I said, he looks after people.'

So how does he look after you? Ashley thought. But she didn't ask, and Joe didn't volunteer anything else. He just padded beside her, all the way home.

Normally, she would have sneaked in round the back way, as usual. But some sort of caution stopped her. She didn't want Joe to see her secret route. Stopping at the front door, she pulled out her key.

'Nice house,' Joe muttered. 'Maybe I'll come round some time.'

Ashley nodded and smiled, putting a finger to her lips. He got the message. With a wave of his hand, he took off into the darkness. Ashley opened the door, very softly, and stepped inside.

Something rustled under her foot.

Pulling the door shut, she bent down and felt the corner of an envelope and she picked it up, peering at the front. But she couldn't see a name, so she pushed it into the pocket of her jeans and began to climb the stairs, slowly and silently. She was desperate to get to bed and sleep, but if she hurried all the boards would creak.

By the time she reached the top, she had almost forgotten about the envelope in her pocket, but it slipped out when she began to undress and she picked it off the floor and opened it.

Inside was a single sheet of paper, folded in four. She unfolded it, and words shouted up at her, written in ugly bubble writing.

CINDY—I KNOW YOU.

JOE
Eddie never explains when he takes up someone new. He just says 'Do this,' or 'Go there' and we find there's another person around.

His mind moves so fast you can't keep up with him. You've got to watch his eyes all the time, the way you'd watch a snake, or a tiger. He's dangerous if he gets bored.

Some of the others don't understand that. They just hang around him because he makes things happen. He gets them living, and doing things they couldn't get together on their own.

I started out like that too. There's always three or

four younger kids tagging on to the crowd, and I was one of those. Eddie let me stick around because my imitations made him laugh. That was the only reason—until that day he decided we were all going to the seaside.

It was very hot. He got a few cars and had us all pile in, and we set off for Margate or somewhere. It was a real laugh, lounging round on the beach and eating ice cream and candy floss.

But then some of them decided to go in the sea in their underwear. They were fooling about and yelling that the water was cold and I could see Eddie looking at me. I knew he wanted some imitations. It was really funny the way those big blokes suddenly shrank when the water hit them.

I knew just how I'd do it, but there was no way I was going to strip down, so I put it off as long as I could. And then I saw that look in his eyes. Annoyed. I thought, Maybe I'd better go along with it, so I went down and played at being Doug, shivering on the waterline. It had them all in fits.

But I kept my T-shirt on.

Eddie didn't say a word. Not then. He just laughed like the others and barracked Doug. But when we were going back, he nodded at me to go in the car with him and Sam. And as soon as we got going he turned round and looked at me.

'Take off that shirt,' he said.

I would have argued, but I knew he'd make me do it in the end, so I stripped off my T-shirt and sat there shivering while he looked at the bruises. That was the time I had a cracked rib as well, and I was purple all down one side.

Sam was watching in the mirror, and I heard her catch her breath, but Eddie didn't say anything for a minute. Then he nodded. 'Put your shirt on again.'

I pulled it over my head, and I was shivering worse now. And not just because the T-shirt was damp.

'He'll hit my mother . . . ' I said.

If you make a fuss. That's what I meant. Eddie just shook his head.

'I'll see to him. He won't lay a finger on her. But you're not going back there.'

I didn't know what he meant, but I had this sudden, wonderful feeling. Like I'd had my fists clenched tight for years and years and all at once I could straighten them. You're not going back there. I never even asked him where I was going instead. Just sat back in a daze and knew it was all right.

Eddie turned back to Sam. 'How about if he goes to your mum?'

Sam didn't look too sure, but Eddie's never wrong about things like that. He always knows what he can ask people. When we turned up at Tricia's house and

I saw her blonde hair and her high heels, I thought, He's crazy. She's not the sort of woman that wants a kid around.

But all he had to do was strip off my shirt. Tricia took one look at the bruises and gave him a long, straight look.

'I'll do whatever you want,' she said.

And that was it. I've been there ever since. The next day, Eddie sent his mate Rick round to photograph my bruises and they posted the pictures to Vince with an anonymous letter.

As long as you treat Gayle right, the police won't get these.

That was all it took. Vince hasn't laid a finger on Mum, from that day to this, and I know I'm safe at Tricia's.

The only thing is—I've got to keep in with Eddie. I've got to make sure he doesn't get bored with me.

7

Ashley didn't fall asleep until it was nearly light. After what seemed like less than an hour's sleep, she was woken by the sound of banging on the front door. 'Ash! Are you there? *Ash!*'

As she opened her eyes, she could hear Pauline, too. Shouting and knocking on the radiator.

'Ashley! Ashie!'

It was half-past eight.

She wasted one more second staring at her watch, and then she shot out of bed, wrenched the curtains apart and opened the window. Down in the street, Vikki stepped backwards to look at her.

'What's the matter?' she called up. 'Are you ill?'

Ashley groaned and shook her head. 'I overslept!'

'But you never oversleep!'

'Well, I did today!' Ashley snapped. 'Don't wait for me.'

She slammed the window shut. And thought, *Vikki doesn't know about the wall. She hasn't been up to the Row yet.* Her mind filled with pictures from the night before. In horrible, clear detail. She saw herself prancing about on the roof of the chippie. Spraying Fat Annie's new white paint. Jumping into a stolen car.

Being in the car when it was wrecked.

She couldn't believe she'd been so crazy. In the mirror, she saw her face, smudged with dirt, and her tumbled, tangled hair. She snatched up the hairbrush and brushed savagely until her scalp tingled. Then she wrenched the whole bunch of hair back into an elastic band.

Pauline was still shouting, in a tired, ragged voice. 'Ashley! What's the matter? I've been calling for hours.'

Wearily, Ashley opened the door and shouted back. 'It's OK. I won't be long.'

It took her three minutes to scrub at her face with a flannel and throw on her school uniform. When she went downstairs, she found Pauline sitting on the end of the bed.

'I was coming up,' she said.

'Oh, sure!' Ashley whisked past and went into the kitchen. She couldn't bear to pretend anything just then. There was enough to cope with. Noisily, she filled the kettle and plugged it in. Then she called down the hall.

'Toast?'

'You haven't got time,' Pauline said. 'You'll be late unless you go straight away, and then—'

'Well, I'm not going yet!' Ashley jammed two slices of bread into the toaster and stuck her head out of the kitchen. 'I'm going to have some breakfast, so you might as well have some too.'

'But there'll be trouble—'

'So? Why not?' Ashley marched down to the front room door and stood there with her hands on her hips, glaring down at her mother. 'Come on. Tell me. Why have *I* got to be so perfect?'

Pauline wavered. 'I'm not asking you to be perfect.'

'Yes you are! You're making a fuss, just because I've overslept. Teenagers oversleep all the time. It's called *adolescence*. Some of the people in my class are only there three days a week. And Lisa rolls in at eleven o'clock sometimes. Why have I got to be different, just because you're ill?'

'It's not that.'

'Oh, *isn't* it?' Ashley said nastily.

The toast popped up, and she marched back to the kitchen, to make the tea with one hand while she buttered the toast with the other. *Just an ordinary morning*, she thought, in a rage. *Get the breakfast. Make a sandwich for Mum's lunch. Wash her. Put her clothes on. That's enough for one person. Why do I have to be better than everyone else as well?*

She was still in a temper as she put the tea and toast on the tray and took it through. Sweeping her mother's magazines away, she banged the tray down on to the bedside table.

65

'We'll have this and then I'll get you dressed.'

Pauline winced and struggled on to the bed. 'You don't need to—'

'Yes I do. I'm going to make sure you're dressed absolutely perfectly. And I'm going to brush your hair till it's like silk. Just in case Janet comes again.' Ashley sliced the toast into fingers and posted one into her mother's mouth, to stop her talking. 'Or do you want her catching you in your nightie two days running?'

Pauline took the toast out. 'She only wants to help. You're not being fair.'

'What's so great about being fair?' Ashley pushed in another piece of toast, while Pauline's mouth was open. Then she gulped down her own tea and went to sort out some clothes. No point in breaking her neck to get to school now. Mrs Prosser would only give her one detention, however late she was.

She was wrong. Mrs Prosser gave her two detentions. One at lunchtime, for being late, and one after school, for forgetting to do her homework. The only good thing about them was that they kept her away from Vikki. By the time Ashley got to school, she'd seen the wall, and heard the rumours, and she kept nagging about it, all day.

'Ash, you're a lunatic. Annie had the police round first thing, and there's going to be terrible trouble. She thinks the person who painted her wall stole the Hyena's car too, and wrote it off.'

Every time they were on their own, she started up again. If it hadn't been for the detentions, Ashley would have gone mad. She actually enjoyed sitting on her own at lunchtime and coming out after school to find the road deserted.

Though it was odd to find it so very deserted.

It was even odder when she walked past the flats and found nobody there, either. People usually hung around by the benches, chatting and eating chips. Where was everyone?

She found out when she reached the Row. Outside Fat Annie's, there was a huge crowd, laughing and shouting. They were all staring up at the roof of the chippie.

The Hyena was up there, with a pot of white paint. He was trying to ignore all the noise, but it wasn't easy. Every time he moved, someone yelled.

'Mind you don't fall!'

'Look out behind you!'

'WHOOPS!'

Vikki was near the back of the crowd. She looked round and beckoned, and Ashley wriggled through to her, scowling.

'Hope he slips off,' she muttered. 'Why couldn't he leave it alone?'

Vikki grinned. 'It's Annie, of course. She made him go up there. Don't you think it's cruel? He's petrified.'

The Hyena's pasty face was stiff with the effort of ignoring all the shouts. He had looped the handle of the paintpot over his arm, so that he could keep a hand against the wall, and he was dipping his brush in and dabbing at the coloured letters with jerky, irregular movements. The 'C' and the 'I' were already blotted out and he was halfway across the 'N'.

Someone at the front began to sing.

One hyena, hanging on the wall.

One hyena, hanging on the wall.

The song swept back through the crowd as everyone else picked it up. *And if one hyena should accidentally FALL—*

They bellowed the word, catching him by surprise, and he tottered and clutched at the wall for support. The paintpot swung wildly, slopping white paint over his trousers and there was a great wave of laughter from below.

Ashley shook her head. 'He's an idiot! Why didn't he do it while we were all in school?'

'I think he was out,' Vikki said. 'He was only just back when I got here, because I heard Annie bawl him out.'

'But she didn't have to make him go straight up there. She's a maniac.'

'She certainly is.' Vikki grinned again and pointed across the road.

Fat Annie was standing in the shop doorway, waving the window pole at the crowd. 'You can stop that!' she bellowed. 'I've had the police round once already, and I'll fetch them round again if you don't clear off! Let Mr Galt get on with his work!'

There was a shriek of laughter from the front. 'Hey, *Mr Galt*! Let's see you fall off the roof!'

One of the boys started a slow handclap. 'Off! Off! Off!'

All around them, people started to pick up the chant, and Vikki nudged Ashley. 'It's getting nasty,' she muttered. 'Let's go.'

Ashley nodded, and they began to work their way through the crush, to the traffic lights. They were almost there when someone pulled at Ashley's sleeve.

'Hi.' It was Joe, with his hands in his pockets and his white clown's face lolling sideways. 'I was looking for you.'

'*Hi!*' said Vikki.

Joe ignored her. He was watching Ashley. 'There's a party tonight.'

'So?' Ashley shrugged.

Vikki nudged her, but she didn't take any notice. She was watching Joe as hard as he was watching her. There were dark hollows under his eyes and his cheekbones were sharp angles. He raised one eyebrow.

'Eddie said I had to bring you.'

'Did he?' Ashley shook her head. 'Well, I don't go to parties.'

Vikki almost exploded with impatience. 'Oh, go on! I'll come with you. It'll be a laugh.'

'You can't come,' Joe said evenly, still looking at Ashley. 'Eddie didn't ask you.'

'And I'm not—' Ashley began.

Joe didn't give her a chance to finish. Without any warning, his face crinkled into a simper and he edged closer and nudged her. 'Go *on*, Ash!'

Ashley stopped, catching her breath, and Joe nudged her again, leering sideways at her. 'Go on. It'll be fantastic!' he said shrilly.

Ashley laughed. She couldn't help herself. Vikki scowled and went bright red.

'Oh, great! You're a real friend, aren't you?'

'I didn't mean—' Ashley said.

But it was too late. Vikki flounced off in a temper, swinging her bag as she went and catching Ashley round the back of the legs.

Joe copied her, swinging his shoulders pettishly.

'Don't,' Ashley said.

'You like it,' Joe said. He was solemn now, staring at her disconcertingly.

'I *don't* like it. Vikki's my friend.'

'So why did you laugh?'

'Because . . . '

Because what? She didn't know. The words shrivelled away and she was left staring at Joe's big, hollow eyes.

Suddenly he smiled. A lop-sided grin that showed his irregular yellow teeth. 'I'll call for you then. Around nine o'clock.'

'But I'm not coming—'

It was too late to argue. Before Ashley could say a word, he had loped off, and she was on her own. Except for the crowd of people shouting up at the roof.

The Hyena had been painting, desperately, all the time she and Joe were talking. He was nearly at the end now, just laying the first streaky white stroke over the 'Y'. His clothes were splashed and stained and his shoulders hunched forward. Ashley couldn't bear to watch him.

She glanced away, towards the chippie. And for a moment she saw a face at an upstairs window. A pale, fat face peering out between the curtains to see what was going on.

Tony Cavalieri.

It was only a glimpse. When he saw Ashley looking up at him, he spun away, vanishing into the darkness of the room behind. That was all anyone ever saw of him now. Since the fight. He peered out at the Row from behind those net curtains, ducking back when anyone noticed him. Briefly, Ashley wondered how much he knew about what went on. Then the lights changed, and she crossed the road and forgot about him.

When she got home, there was another envelope lying on the mat. The same sort of envelope as yesterday's, with nothing written on the front. She scooped it up quickly, weighing it in her hand.

'Ashley?' her mother called. She sounded nervous and tentative.

'I'll be there in a minute,' Ashley called back. 'Wait till you hear what's going on up at the shop!'

As she spoke, she was opening the envelope. It was the same as the last one, with bubble writing in spidery blue biro. But there were more words.

CINDY, they said. I KNOW YOU. YOU THINK YOU'RE SUCH A GYMNAST, DON'T YOU? BUT ONE DAY YOU'RE GOING TO FALL.

ANNIE GALT
I don't know who that CINDY is, but if I get hold of her I'll wring her neck.

This used to be a decent neighbourhood. When Barry was alive, the customers were our friends. They respected us. Now they're all out for themselves. I can't relax for a minute.

The children are terrors for shoplifting. Whatever I'm up to, I have to keep an eye on that video screen, and even then we lose about twenty pounds' worth of stuff a week.

The women are almost as bad. They don't shoplift— not most of them—but they're always moaning about the prices. And then there's the lads who want to smash the place up in the evenings. And the winos who'd fall asleep in the doorway if you let them.

Spider Mo camped out here for a week one winter. The police were useless. However much I complained, she was there again the next night. I had to act quite nasty before she got the message.

'Eddie told me it was a good place,' she kept muttering. She can't cope with more than one idea a day. 'Eddie said I'd be safe here. Better than on the estate. Said it was warmer.'

If Eddie Beale wants to keep her warm, he can buy her a sleeping bag. I knew what he was up to, and I wasn't going to let him get away with it. If my shop gets associated with people like her, I'll start losing customers.

I tried helping her along with my foot, but she just

shifted a bit and crept back while I wasn't looking. So in the end I sent Geoff down, with a bucket of water.

He needed nagging, of course. When I looked out of the front window, he was standing there dithering. Looking down at the bundle of rags and old newspapers as if he didn't know there was a person in the middle.

I leaned out of the window and yelled at him. 'Just do it. Or you'll be spending the night out there with her.'

Even then he didn't do it on purpose. But he stepped back to look up at me, and the water slopped out of the bucket, all over Mo's bedding.

It worked like a charm. She sat up and swore at him, and then started gathering the whole lot up, just the way I'd meant her to. If I'd been down there, I would have given her another dose, to help her on her way, but Geoffrey just stood there like a dummy.

He's always let people push him around, ever since he was a little boy. The way he watched Mo shuffling across the road, you'd have thought he wanted our doorstep cluttered up with rubbish like that.

I was going to give him an earful when he came in, but he went straight past the living room and locked himself in his bedroom, so I couldn't get at him.

He doesn't realize how much the place has gone downhill. He was just a little boy when this was a nice respectable neighbourhood, and he's got used to the vandalism and the gangs and the terrible language. He hasn't got any idea of how to hit back. When he saw his car last night, he just cried.

Sometimes I feel so lonely I could scream. But it's no good giving in to that. If Geoffrey won't fight back, I'll have to do it myself. And the first person I'm going to get is that Cindy. She's the last straw. I wish she'd fallen off the roof.

8

Ashley stared down at the paper in her hand and tried to stay calm. Who could have sent it? And how did he know about her?

Pauline called again. 'Ash?'

Roughly, Ashley screwed up the paper, pushing it into her pocket, out of sight. Then she arranged a cheerful smile on her face and went into the front room.

'Hi. Sorry I'm late. I got a detention because of oversleeping, but it was OK. How about you?'

Her mother hesitated.

Ashley sat down on the end of the bed. 'I'm sorry I was a pig this morning.'

'It's not your fault.' Pauline looked down at her hands. 'I'm not being fair, am I? You've got too much to do.'

Ashley knew what that meant. 'You've been talking to Janet, haven't you? What did she do? Phone? Come round?'

'She did phone, but that's not why—'

'Oh no?' Ashley pulled a face. 'I bet I can guess what she said. She talked about me, didn't she? Said I'm looking peaky. And she's *horribly afraid* that I'm missing out on things. Not leading a normal life.'

'Well, it's true, isn't it?' Pauline said. 'You are missing out. Louise and Karen are always going to parties and having fun and—'

'You think I want to go to parties like that? To eat jelly and play Pass the Parcel?'

That raised a grin, but only for a moment. Then Pauline was frowning again. 'You know what I mean. You don't do anything any more. You've even stopped going to gymnastics. You ought to be mixing with people. Building up your confidence—'

'There's nothing wrong with my confidence. Or my friends. In fact—' (Ashley had an inspiration.) '—I was asked to a party tonight.'

'Tonight?' Pauline blinked. 'Well, that's a bit sudden, but—'

'Don't worry. I'm not going.'

The moment the words were out, Ashley knew she'd blundered. Pauline sat up sharply and two bright pink spots flamed on her cheeks.

'You see? That's how it always is! You say no to everything, just because of me.'

'It's not because of you. Don't be a moron.'

'I'm not a moron! And I'm not a baby, either. I don't need minding. You're going to that party, or I'll phone Janet up and tell her she's right, and we can't manage on our own.'

'Mum—'

'Shut up! I don't want to hear it. Go and do your homework and then sort yourself out some nice clothes.'

Ashley considered arguing, took another look at her mother's face and ditched the idea. It wasn't worth the hassle. Pauline wasn't going to give in, whatever she said. She'd just have to go to the party and put up with it.

If Joe turned up.

He turned up all right. Bang on the dot of nine. When Ashley opened the front door, he was lolling against the wall, and he stepped inside and into the front room without being asked.

'Hi,' he said.

'Hallo.' Pauline sat up straighter in her armchair and gave him a bright, determined smile. Then she looked at Ashley and frowned. 'Couldn't you find anything better than those old jeans? What about your blue dress?'

'Jeans,' Joe said. 'That's what she ought to wear.'

Ashley wondered why, but she didn't waste time asking. She picked up her jacket. 'Bye, Mum. I won't be very late—'

'You be as late as you want to be!' Pauline said fiercely. 'I'll be really angry if you get back too early!'

'What a great mother!' Joe grinned at Ashley. 'Think she'd adopt me?'

'No chance!' Ashley said. 'If I want a brother, I'll knit one.' She pushed him out of the room and opened the front door. 'Which way are we going?'

Joe stepped past her and set off down the road, away from the Row. 'Industrial estate.'

'For a party?' Ashley had to jog to catch him up. 'What are you talking about?'

'There's a great warehouse. No one goes down there at night. Only the winos, and we can handle them.'

'What sort of party is this?'

'You'll see.'

Ashley wasn't sure she wanted to see, but she knew her mother would go crazy if she went home. So she trailed after Joe, imagining noise and drugs in an echoing forest of steel shelving.

There was plenty of noise when they got there— they could hear the music halfway across the estate— but there was no shelving. Only a big, empty space, with a stack of boxes at one end and dozens of people standing around drinking and talking.

Not dancing.

Ashley wondered why for a moment, and then she realized that most of the people were men.

'Where's the girls?' she said.

Joe half-closed his eyes. 'Not that sort of party,

mate,' he grunted. His voice rumbled in his chest. 'Eddie's parties are different. OK? No hangers on.' He flexed his shoulders, as if he had huge muscles, and stuck his thumbs into the pockets of his jeans.

Ashley looked round, wondering who he was being. Across the warehouse she saw Doug, with his shoulders flexed and one thumb in his pocket.

Joe grunted again. 'Eddie does things his way, mate. You don't get asked to his parties unless you're on the firm.'

Ashley looked round again. 'So which one's Eddie, then?'

Joe stopped being Doug and stared at her. 'What do you mean? He's not here yet.'

'How was I supposed to know? I've never seen him.'

Joe stared again, and then shrugged. 'You will. When he turns up, you'll know all right.'

It was eleven o'clock before that happened. By then, Ashley was bored rigid. Some of the men had been out and bought chips, but no one had offered her any, and she didn't fancy the beer Joe had brought her. She was sitting all on her own in a corner, playing with a little dog who'd popped up from nowhere. Wondering if it was late enough to go home.

Suddenly, there was a blast of cold air. She looked up and saw a couple of men pushing the big warehouse door open. Outside there were blazing headlights and the sound of a car revving impatiently.

As the door swung open, the car edged forward, right into the warehouse. People fell away on each side and it came to a stop in the middle of them. No one said a word. The only noise was the music which was still blaring away, sounding thin and cheap in the glare of the headlights.

Is it him? Ashley wanted to say. *Is it Eddie?* But Joe wasn't near, and she was afraid to ask anyone else.

Doug walked over to the passenger's door, still holding his paper of chips. 'Hallo, mate!' he said. 'Thought you'd decided to give it a miss.'

Ashley couldn't hear the answer from inside, but she found herself holding her breath as Doug gripped the door handle with one huge hand and swung the door open. And she had a curious feeling that all the others were holding their breath as well. Waiting for someone (for Eddie—it had to be Eddie) to get out of the car.

Then he did, and the first thing Ashley thought was, *He's so small!*

She'd been expecting someone huge. Bigger than Doug, and rippling with tattoos. But he was no more than average height. A wiry man in jeans and a T-shirt, with an ugly, uneven face.

He walked round to the other side of the car and opened the door. Sam was leaning back in the driver's seat and she swivelled sideways, sticking out one long leg. Then she stood up, in a single, fluid movement. She was wearing something short and glittering, and very high heels.

For a party in a warehouse?

Ashley thought it was weird, but everyone else started to cheer, parting to make way for her. Sam walked between them, like a model on a catwalk, following the wide beam of light thrown by the car's headlamps.

At the far end she stopped, without turning, and the cheering voices stopped too. Again, Ashley sensed that curious, breathless feeling. As though all the men were expecting something to happen. She could see Joe opposite, with his eyes fixed on the back of Sam's glittering dress.

'Hey,' said Eddie.

His voice was not loud, but the word was an order. Ashley could hear that. An order from someone who doesn't expect to be disobeyed. Sam turned. Her face was very pale in the headlights and the front of her dress rippled and glittered as she breathed, quickly and nervously.

'What do you want?' she said. The words were sharp.

Eddie raised one hand, holding out a glass bottle, full of some colourless liquid. With her eyes on the bottle, Sam came down the beam of light again to face him. He gave her the bottle and she pulled out the cork with her teeth. Someone switched off the music and the silence was abrupt.

Eddie bent sideways, lifting something out of the car. It was a heavy stick, with one end wrapped in cloth. Still staring at Sam, he pulled a lighter out of his pocket and flicked it on. The little flame licked at the wrapped cloth and it flared alight, burning with a smell of paraffin.

Eddie snapped the lighter off and dropped it into his pocket. Then he handed the stick to Sam and stepped back. She stood for a moment, studying the flames as all the men edged away too, leaving her alone in the centre of the warehouse.

Even then, Ashley hadn't realized what was going to happen. She moved back with the rest, watching Sam and the flame and the bottle. Beyond, she could see Joe. He was staring hard, with his mouth open and beads of sweat around his nostrils.

Lifting the bottle, Sam took a long swig, holding the

liquid in her mouth. Then she raised the blazing stick high into the air. In that instant, Ashley guessed.

She can't—

Tilting her head back, Sam brought the stick slowly down towards her face. The flames flickered as her hand shook, but she didn't stop. Until, suddenly, she opened her mouth and breathed out a stream of fire.

It roared like dragon's breath, right across the warehouse, with men leaping away on each side. Ashley could feel the heat from where she was standing.

Sam raised the bottle again. No one made a sound. Joe had closed his eyes and Ashley could see him inhaling, very slowly, like someone afraid to disturb the air.

Sam poured the rest of the liquid into her mouth, raised the burning torch and tilted her head back again. Then she breathed again. This time, the fire shot out in a great tongue, up towards the roof. Its light glinted on the sequins of her dress and turned her hair scarlet. For a split second, she seemed to be all fire.

Then she laughed and tossed the empty bottle high into the air.

Eddie caught it. He weighed it in his hands for a second then threw it on, straight at Joe.

'Here! Catch!'

DOUG

Everyone does tricks for Eddie. Don't know how he does it, but he's always one step ahead.

We go back a long way, me and him. Been best mates since we were kids. He may not be as big as me, but don't let that fool you. He's hard. And he's got brains, too. I've never seen him put down, and we've been in some tight corners together.

Like that job we did a couple of years ago. Tony Cavalieri was still on his feet then, and his gang lifted a load of DVD players and stashed them away in a lock-up garage. I don't know how Eddie got the tip-off, but he comes up behind me in the pub at lunchtime and mutters in my ear.

'What would you say to a hundred brand new DVD players? Been lifted already, so they can't squeal. All we've got to do is wire a van and load them up.'

'We taking Phil?' I say. Like—we usually did. But Eddie wasn't having any of that.

'Just you and me. OK? And don't tell a soul.'

So that night we go out looking for a likely van and pick up one around Nettles Hill. Nice and anonymous, and a full petrol tank. And when we get to the garage, it looks a dream. End of a blind alley, with blank walls on both sides. No reason for anyone to come by. All we've got to do is back up and load the DVD players in.

I start on that and while I'm hauling the boxes, Eddie's poking round the back of the garage. Then suddenly—we hear the cars. Two of them.

They turn down the alley and line up side by side, blocking the way out. Blinding us with their lights. We hear the doors go, and a lot of feet. I had a blade in my pocket—you've got to have something—but Eddie smacked my hand away from it.

'Cut that out. Get into the van and put the headlights on.'

So I crawl round and knock the door open. When I turn on the headlights, I can see there's half a dozen blokes coming towards us. Big and ugly.

They didn't like the headlights and one of them starts yelling at me to turn them off, but Eddie's down by my feet hissing about the radio. To turn the radio on really loud.

Sounds stupid, but I do what he says and then he's pulling at my ankle to get me out again. When I land up beside him, I can see he's got his mobile phone out.

He's calling the police.

I thought he'd really cracked up, but he comes off the phone and he's humming to himself. I've fixed them. I've fixed the bastards ... *And I want to say,* Yes, but you've fixed us too, *but there's no time because we can hear the sirens already.*

Three police cars screech across the end of the road, blocking the whole lot of us in. It looks like the end, and I'm sweating cobs, but Eddie doesn't turn a hair. Suddenly he's on his feet, throwing stones. One, two, three, four. And not a single miss. He knocked out all the Cavalieris' headlights, and suddenly we're the ones behind the light. The ones nobody can see.

'Come on!' Eddie goes.

He drags me back into the garage and suddenly I see there's a roof panel missing. And Phil's leaning through the hole, waiting to pull us up.

He had a van in the yard on the other side. In thirty seconds we were away, and the police never had a chance of catching us.

And the real joke was that Phil and Shaun had been lifting the DVD players all the time we were having that stand-off with the Cavalieris. We got away with twenty of them and made half a grand. I was just a decoy.

Like I said, everyone does tricks for Eddie.

9

'Catch!' said Eddie. And he threw the bottle straight at Joe.

Joe reacted like lightning, stretching into the air, and catching the bottle one-handed.

The moment his fingers touched it, Eddie picked a beer can off the ground and shied that at him. And then another one. Ashley couldn't believe Joe was going to catch them, but he did more than catch.

Before the first can reached him, he sent the bottle spinning into the air. That left him free to catch the beer cans. And when the bottle came down, the cans went up.

He was juggling.

He moved forward, into the circle of people that had formed round Eddie and Sam. When he was standing in front of Eddie, he let the first can spin out of the dance and dropped it neatly at Eddie's feet. Then he did the same with the second one.

Giving the bottle a final, dizzying throw, he caught it by the neck and held it out to Sam.

'Pretty good,' Eddie said. He leaned over to Doug and grabbed the sausage out of his chip paper. 'Here.'

It looked like a reward and Ashley thought the

show was over. But suddenly the little dog from nowhere bounded forward into the circle, rearing on to its hind legs and strutting towards the sausage. It whined on a long, pitiful note.

Eddie looked down at it and a long, slow grin spread across his face. Then he looked back at Joe.

'Nice sausage,' Sam said quickly. She reached out to snatch it away, but she wasn't fast enough. Eddie jerked it out of her reach, without taking his eyes off Joe's face.

There was a split second's pause and then Joe stepped forward, holding his arms high on his chest and letting his hands droop. Like a dog begging. Slowly, on stiff legs, he edged up to Eddie.

'Sausage?' he said.

He was mimicking the dog, holding his head on one side, with an eager, Jack Russell look. Doug started laughing.

But Eddie didn't laugh. He held the sausage higher, waving it from side to side.

'Dance for it.'

Joe began to totter round clumsily, with his mouth open and his tongue hanging out sideways. Everyone was laughing now. Eddie jerked the sausage upwards, and Joe leaped awkwardly after it, whining just like the dog.

It was horrible. Ashley didn't know why, but she

screwed up her fists, so hard that the nails dug into her palms.

Eddie kept Joe jumping on and on, until all the men were roaring with laughter and Joe was completely out of breath. It looked as if he would have to give in and collapse, but, at the very last moment, Eddie nodded sharply.

'Die for the Queen!'

Flopping to the ground, Joe rolled over like a dog, arms and legs bent and red mouth open wide. With a casual, scornful gesture, Eddie flipped the sausage into his open mouth, and Joe scrambled up, chewing as he walked back towards Ashley.

Avoiding her eyes.

Behind him, the circle began to shrink, but the movement was reluctant. The men were looking about, as if they wanted something else to happen.

'What about the girl?' one of them said. 'Does she do anything?'

Ashley didn't realize that he meant her until Eddie turned towards her. Suddenly, she caught the full force of his stare. He didn't say a word, but she found herself stepping into the middle of the circle.

It was ridiculous. There was no point in making a fool of herself. What could she possibly do that wouldn't be an anti-climax, after the juggling and the fire-eating?

She almost stepped back again. And then Eddie raised one eyebrow, enquiringly. *So?* said his look. *What's your speciality?*

Suddenly, doing nothing wasn't an option. It wasn't the men standing round who made the decision for her. It was Eddie. He was staring at her, waiting for some kind of show. If she didn't come up with a performance, she didn't count.

And there *was* something she could do. Of course there was.

'I do this!' she said loudly. Purposely dramatic. Without giving anyone time to react, she launched herself forward into a chain of cartwheels. Head-over-feet-over-head-over-feet-over-head-over-feet-over-head—

She took the gamble that the circle would part for her, and so it did, just in time, with men shoving each other out of the way to avoid being knocked by her flying legs. She cartwheeled all the way up to the far end of the warehouse in an unbroken, spinning sequence.

As she turned to come back, she was working out the timing in her head. If she aimed slightly more to the left, she thought she could end up standing to attention, right in front of Eddie. She glanced at him once and then flung herself forward.

Each time she flipped over, her eyes found his

face. He stood there waiting for her, with the same attentive, half-amused look as he'd had while he watched Sam and Joe.

Until the final cartwheel. Suddenly, just before she went into that, he tilted his head and stepped sideways. Ashley found herself facing the long, gleaming car. And instantly, as though it had leapt from his mind into hers, she had a vision of herself sailing right over the top of the car.

It was a dare. He had dared her to do it.

She had no idea whether it was possible, and there was no time to work it out. If she got the timing wrong, she would crash straight into the windscreen and break it. And probably injure herself, as well.

But—

Going into the last cartwheel, she saw Eddie staring at her, and she knew she was going to do it.

She went over and her feet came down (right, left) exactly in front of the car. Without hesitating, her hands smacked on to the bonnet (left, right) and up she went, on to the roof. Her feet touched down again (right, left) pushing her up and over into a last flip that took her clear of the back of the car. She landed neatly, with her feet almost together, and the warehouse exploded into cheers.

It was more than she'd ever dreamt she could do. She was speechless with the excitement of it. It was better than painting the best wall she'd ever imagined, in her wildest dreams. She stood in the middle of the cheers with triumph singing in her head.

Eddie didn't say a word. He didn't even smile. He just picked a handful of chips out of Doug's paper and walked round the car, holding them out to her like a bouquet. But she couldn't take one. She couldn't even speak.

It was well after midnight when she got back home. As she walked into the house, the phone started ringing.

She ran into the front room.

'I wouldn't answer it,' Pauline said. 'Not at this time of night.'

But Ashley had already snatched up the receiver. 'Yes? Who's that?'

There was an odd kind of mutter at the other end of the line. A man's voice, not a woman's.

'Hallo?' Ashley said. 'Who is it?'

There was another mutter. Then the voice whispered down the line, faint and distorted.

' Cindeee . . . '

'What?' Ashley heard her own voice rise.

There was a rustling, crackling noise, like someone crumpling paper, and the voice whispered again.

'. . . Cindee . . . you'll never keep it up . . . you'll lose your balance . . . '

'What?' Ashley's hand began to shake.

'. . . you know I'm right . . . there's going to be trouble . . . '

Sharply, Ashley put the receiver down. Her right hand was shaking so much that she had to put the left one over it, to steady it.

'Who was it?' Pauline said.

'I don't — I couldn't hear properly.' Ashley's voice came out sounding normal, but she didn't dare turn round for a moment. 'I'll just check the number.'

She tapped in the call-tracing code, but the message she expected came back.

'You were called . . . today . . . at . . . one twenty-five. The caller withheld their number . . . Please hang up . . . please hang up . . . '

Slowly she lowered the receiver, trying to be calm. It didn't matter. It was only a phone call.

But the words came spinning back at her . . . *you'll get into trouble . . .* Someone was trying to scare her.

Well, she wasn't going to be scared. Snapping the receiver down into its cradle, she turned to her mother.

'OK, Mum? Had a good evening? You must be really tired.'

'I'm fine,' Pauline said. 'What was the phone call?'

'Wrong number,' Ashley said briskly. 'Want me to make you a drink before we go to bed?'

But she was still shaking as she went into the kitchen. The same questions kept running round and round in her head. *Who is it? And how does he know about me?*

MRS MACDONALD
Phone calls! At this time of night!

It woke me up, and I'm sure it woke them up, as well. You'd think people would be more considerate. There's Pauline in the state she's in, and that poor wee girl with school to go to. They need their sleep.

Especially Ashley. I don't know how she does it. She goes up the road to do her shopping like a proper little housewife. Not like the rest of the young people around here. There are some wild ones, I can tell you. You've only got to look at the graffiti. And the vandalism. I've heard them joyriding up and down the Row at three o'clock in the morning, keeping decent people from their sleep.

They ought to take a leaf out of wee Ashley's book. She's like a little angel, with that fair hair and those lovely manners. Good morning, Mrs Macdonald *she says when she sees me.* How's the arthritis? *And she waits for an answer, too. Not like some people.*

I'm not saying it's right, mind. A girl like her, having

to look after her mother, all on her own. What's the rest of the family thinking about? Even the Cavalieris do better than that. They've really rallied round to look after poor Tony, since he had that terrible accident. When I see Ashley struggling up the road with three bags of shopping, I want to give that aunt of hers a piece of my mind.

People just won't accept their responsibilities, these days.

10

'Vik,' Ashley said. 'What would you do if you got an anonymous letter?'

They were standing in the lunch queue on Monday. Ashley made the question sound as offhand as she could, but Vikki turned round sharply.

'Someone's sending you anonymous letters?'

Thanks, Vik. Now there were half a dozen people staring at them. Ashley tried to pass it off as a joke.

'It's a nightmare! There's this little fat man with glasses and green spots. Keeps writing love letters in shaving foam on my front door.'

Vikki gave her a long look, but she got the message. She let out a loud, delighted shriek. 'You're so *lucky*! Love letters *and* free shaving foam. What're you complaining about? He's probably a millionaire.'

Ashley picked up a tray. 'Don't care if he's a zillionaire three times over. He can't spell. He keeps calling me his "little purple pinnapple".'

'That's gross!' Vikki pulled a face and held out her plate for chips. 'Shall I sort him out? Does he like brunettes too?'

She kept the joke running, but Ashley knew that

wouldn't be the end. Vikki would make sure she found out what was going on.

She did. When they came out of school, she dawdled on purpose, to give Lisa the slip, and she sent Matt away, even though he'd waited twenty minutes for her.

'I'll come round later. OK? I need to talk to Ashley just now.'

'Aw, Vikki!'

Matt was annoyed. Ashley saw the back of his neck turn bright red. But Vikki didn't take any notice of that. She prodded him in the chest and looked up at him sternly.

'You don't own me, you know. Go home and ask Ginger to cut your hair. I'll see you at seven.'

Even though Matt was twice her size, she always got her own way. He muttered a bit, but he went off obediently, saying, 'Mind you're not late.'

Vikki sighed and picked up her bag. 'Boys!'

'Matt's OK,' Ashley said. 'That was pretty mean, you know.'

'Rubbish! If he had things his way, he'd never let me talk to anyone else.' Vikki started off down the road. 'Now what's all this about anonymous letters? How many have you had?'

Ashley felt stupid. 'It's not really worth fussing about.'

'Don't give me that. It's bugging you. You know I can always tell.'

It was true. That was why they were friends. They always knew about each other.

Ashley looked down at her feet. 'I've had two letters. And yesterday there was a phone call. But none of them said anything really. Only —'

'Only?'

'Only he called me Cindy.'

Vikki stopped. 'But you said no one knew except me.'

'That's right.' Ashley hesitated. But she had to ask it. 'You haven't told anyone, have you?'

'Of course I haven't!' Vikki said. Then she went pink. 'Well . . . only Matt.'

'But you promised!'

'Matt doesn't count. I said I'd never speak to him again if he told anyone. He won't say anything.'

'I suppose not,' Ashley said. But it took an effort.

'I reckon you ought to phone the police.'

'Are you mad?' Ashley rolled her eyes. 'What do I say? *It's like this, officer. I was just standing on the roof of the chippie, spraying my name on a wall . . . ?*'

'They wouldn't worry about that.'

'You want to bet? And what about that car crash? You said Annie was out for someone's blood for that.'

'Oh. Yes.' Vikki pulled a face. 'I told you you were crazy to get mixed up in that.'

'Well, I did,' Ashley said. Meaning, *And shut up about it.* 'So I can't go near the police. Anyway, there's nothing to show them. Just a couple of little notes.'

'Maybe there'll be something else today. Something in the post.' Vikki started getting excited. 'I'll come home with you and see, shall I?'

It was no good saying no. That sort of thing never put her off. Ashley looked wary. 'You're not to tell my mum . . .'

''Course I won't. What d'you think I am?' Vikki could hardly wait. She darted across the Row when the lights changed, and she was almost running when they reached Ashley's house.

Ashley unlocked the door and Vikki pushed her forward, leaning over her shoulder to see if there was anything on the doormat. The moment she was inside, she swooped forward, snatching up the envelopes.

Then she read them, and her face fell. 'It's all junk mail. Except this postcard. Here.'

Ashley took the postcard and called to Pauline. 'Hi! Have you had a good day?' It couldn't have been very good. Not if Pauline hadn't even fetched the post. But at least Janet hadn't been. 'There's a postcard from Karen and Louise!'

They sent one at least once a week, and this one was

typical. A photo of a red London bus. Ashley could just imagine Janet choosing it. *Let's have something cheerful for Mummy, shall we? Time we sent her some news.*

Karen and Louise didn't manage much in the way of news. Just one stiff little sentence each. *Dear Mum, I went to my dancing lesson and my teacher says I'm really good, love Karen.* And *We've got a new hamster, his name is George, love Louise.* Ashley took the card into the front room and Vikki trailed behind her, leafing through the junk mail to double-check that there was nothing exciting mixed up with it.

'Hallo, Vikki,' Pauline said. 'How was school?'

Vikki groaned dramatically. 'It was horrendous! You can't imagine! Mrs Burton had us reading poetry out loud. *O wild West Wind, thou breath of Autumn's being!*' She rolled her eyes and clutched her forehead.

Ashley left them to it, and went to put the kettle on. Vikki didn't come round very often, but she was good value when she did. In thirty seconds, there were giggles coming from the front room, and before the kettle boiled she could hear her mother laughing out loud. Vikki was declaiming at the top of her voice.

'Wild Spirit, which art moving everywhere;

'Destroyer and preserver; hear, O hear!'

That was when the doorbell rang.

Vikki leapt to answer it, before Ashley was even

out of the kitchen. 'Hallo?' they heard her say. And then, 'You've got what?'

She put her head back inside and called down the hall. 'There's a van here, Ash. And someone with a DVD player.'

'What?' Ashley put the teapot down and went along the hall. A middle-aged woman was standing there with a folded piece of paper in one hand. She had a short skirt and very bleached hair, but she looked friendly.

'Ashley?' she said. 'Message from Eddie.'

'I . . . um . . . ' Ashley didn't know what to say. 'Do you want to come in?'

'Thanks. Here.' The woman pushed the paper into Ashley's hand and stepped inside. 'I'd like to meet your mum. Joe says she's good fun.'

Ashley blinked. 'Joe?'

'He lives with me. I'm Tricia, Sam's mother.' The woman walked past her, into the front room, grinning at Pauline. 'Hi,' she said.

Vikki nudged Ashley. 'What does the note say?'

It was quite short, scrawled in heavy, energetic capitals.

YOU WOULDN'T TAKE THE CHIPS, SO I'VE SENT A DVD PLAYER INSTEAD. I ALWAYS PAY FOR GOOD PERFORMANCES.

EDDIE.

'Wah-hey!' Vikki said. 'Must have been *some* performance!'

'Don't be stupid.' Ashley snatched the note away. 'I just did some cartwheels when I went to that party. It wasn't anything much.'

Vikki snorted. 'I thought you'd given up gymnastics. Except on people's roofs.'

'Shut up!' Ashley hissed.

She looked over Vikki's shoulder. Doug was lifting a black DVD player out of the van. And, in the front room, Tricia was talking to her mother.

' . . . it's only an old thing, but Joe said you hadn't got one, and we thought you might be able to use it . . . '

TRICIA
Eddie loves giving people presents. If you do something for him, there's always a little knock on the door next day. After I took Joe in, he sent me flowers for a week.

I knew he was right for Sam, from the moment she met him. Until then, I was really worried about her. She was so wild.

I may not be your conventional mother, with a husband in the house and dinner on the table every night, but I do have some standards. It was getting so I didn't know where Sam was, from one day to the

103

next. And she lost that nice little job she had, in the florist's, because she couldn't be bothered to turn up for work. It was getting so every time I saw her we had a screaming match, with me saying, 'If you carry on like this, you'll be living on the street before you're thirty!'

And she'd just yell back at me. 'Better than being like you, you old cow! Think I want to land up like you, with everyone laughing at me for dressing twenty years too young? And all the women locking their husbands up when I walk past?'

She's always known how to hurt me. At least I've stuck to one man at a time. Until she met Eddie, she was running three or four at once, and I could hear her telling lies to them down the phone. 'No, I can't make it tomorrow. I've got to work late.' Or see my grandmother. Or visit my best friend who's got cancer. She'd say anything. She just didn't care.

And then Eddie brought her home that night and she came in through the door looking as if she'd dropped off a star. Stunned. Glowing. Didn't say a word. Just made herself a cup of coffee and made me one too (and she hadn't done that since she was ten). After that, she finished with everyone else. She was in every night, waiting for the phone to ring, or the knock on the door.

Eddie even got her back to work. They were sitting in the flat one evening, and I heard him say, 'You ought

*to get yourself some modelling or something. To keep
you busy when I don't need you around. Want me to
look out for something?'*

*And the next thing you know, she's working with
that friend of Eddie's. Rick. And she's buying great
clothes and treating me too.*

*Of course, I don't see her as much as I used to.
Sometimes she's off for days at a time, but I never
worry, because she's with Eddie.*

*And anyway, I've got Joe to look after now. Poor
boy. He's not really much more than a child and that
man had been knocking him about for years. I don't
understand how people can do that to children, do
you? If Eddie hadn't rescued him, I reckon he'd be
dead by now. He's a real scream. Keeps you in fits of
laughter, taking people off. (He's great at doing Sam,
actually, but we never let anyone else see that. It's our
little secret.)*

*'Course, it's made a difference to my life, having
him around. It's not cheap, keeping a boy that age.
But Eddie slips me a bit of money now and again,
so that's all right. It's not as much as I'd get if I was
fostering Joe properly, but, as Eddie says, we don't
want the Social Services poking their noses in.*

*There's a lot of cooking to do. Joe needs feeding
properly, to build him up, and I can never tell when
Eddie's going to drop him home. It doesn't hurt a*

kid to stay off school once in a while, but sometimes they're really late.

Still, he's with Eddie, so I don't make a fuss. And I never mind running errands for Eddie, either. Like delivering that DVD player. He said not to tell Pauline it came from him, in case the girl hadn't told her about the party, so I kept my mouth shut. I don't like secrets, but I always keep Eddie's.

I'll do anything for him, as long as he treats Sam right.

11

It was almost an hour before Tricia left. By the time she had finished chatting, they knew all about Sam's modelling triumphs. *I'm so grateful to Eddie for getting her interested. And Rick, as well. Rick's absolutely made Sam's career. You should see some of the pictures he's taken . . .*

Doug had obviously heard it all before. He spent the time setting up the DVD player and tuning it in.

The moment they left, Vikki started nagging at Ashley to go out and hire a DVD.

'You might as well test it out properly.'

Ashley wasn't convinced. 'We don't have to do it today.'

'Oh, come on! What's the point of having a DVD player if you never watch anything?'

'But we've only just got it—'

'That's when you ought to try it out,' Vikki had said firmly. 'Isn't that right, Pauline? Think of all those great films Ashley's missed. It's time she started catching up, isn't it?'

Ashley expected her mother to say no. But she didn't. She was looking remarkably lively and cheerful.

'Go on, Ashie,' she said. 'It would be fun. You could go and get one from that shop next to Annie's.'

'That's right.' Vikki jumped up. 'Ravinder said the new ones were coming in today. Let's go and look them over.'

Ashley gave in. She stood up too. 'All right. But only one.'

Vikki grabbed her arm and almost dragged her out of the house. Ashley couldn't understand what was so great about borrowing some old DVD. It wasn't until they were out in the street that she realized that the DVD was only an excuse. What Vikki really wanted was a chance to talk about Eddie Beale.

'You're *so lucky*!' she said. 'If he's looking after you, you'll never need to worry about anything. Ever again.'

'He's not "looking after" me,' Ashley said crossly. She still wasn't sure how she felt about the DVD player. 'He just—'

'Of course he's looking after you!' Vikki was too impatient and excited to listen. 'You know what you ought to do? You ought to tell him about those anonymous letters.'

Ashley wasn't having any of that. 'Don't be silly. They're not that important.'

'Of course they're important. You never know what he might do next.'

'How d'you know it's a he?'

Vikki snorted. 'Not going to be a woman, is it? It's some weird old man. He'll get nastier and nastier, and then he'll start threatening you, and you won't be able to go out on your own in case you meet him, and—'

'Come on!' Ashley began to laugh. Vikki was always launching into stories like that. 'This is real life, you know, not a horror film. And there's nothing I can do, anyway. If I go to the police, *I'm* the one who's likely to get into trouble. They aren't going to take any notice of those notes.'

'No,' said Vikki. 'That's why you ought to go to Eddie.'

Ashley shook her head, stubbornly. 'I couldn't.'

'Why not? If he likes you enough to give you a DVD player, he'll help you. That's how he is. He looks after his friends.'

'But I'm not his friend.'

Vikki scowled. 'Oh, all right! *Don't* listen to me!'

She started walking again, fast and fiercely. Ashley could see that she was upset, and she jogged a little, to catch up.

'Look. I'm not being difficult. Honestly. It's just . . . well . . . there's not enough to bother him with.'

'And if something else happens?' Vikki said quickly.

'Well, then, I might—'

'Ask Eddie?'

'If you really think he'd do something.'

'I don't think he would. I *know*.' Vikki relaxed and grinned at Ashley. 'So that's settled, then. If anything else happens, we'll go round to Eddie's together and tell him all about it.'

That wasn't quite what Ashley had meant, but they had reached the shops and she didn't want anyone to overhear them. She let it go, and pulled her purse out of her pocket.

'How much is this DVD going to be?'

'I'll treat you,' Vikki said grandly.

She swept into the shop and began to work her way along the shelves, pulling boxes down as she went.

'This is a good one. Really scary. And this is good, too. It made Lisa scream. Oh, and how about this . . . ?'

She collected half a dozen and held them out. Ashley pulled a face.

'How can I choose? I don't know about any of them.'

'It's only like picking a book. Go on. Look at the front of the box.'

Ashley studied the pictures, but before she could settle on anything, Vikki gave a shriek and darted across the shop.

'No! *This* is the one you ought to have! Look!'

She pulled out a box which showed a beautiful blonde walking down the street. Her eyes were big and scared and behind her, ostentatiously lurking, was a man in an overcoat. His shadow fell forwards, on to the path in front of her, and scarlet letters screamed over his head. *Street Stalker*. Vikki put back all the other DVDs and took that one to the counter, pulling Ashley along with her.

'Hi, Rav. We'll take this.'

Behind them, one of the other customers looked up. Ashley heard him draw in his breath sharply. Then a familiar voice said, 'I don't think—'

It was the Hyena. He came up to the counter and peered at the box in Vikki's hand, checking the DVD. His face crumpled into an expression of distaste.

'What's the matter?' Vikki said belligerently. 'Have you got a problem?'

The Hyena went pink. 'I . . . I don't think . . . ' he said awkwardly. 'I mean . . . um . . . it's not a very pleasant subject, is it? Stalking?' He looked at Ashley. 'Your mother might not like—'

'Pauline's OK,' Vikki said tartly. '*She* knows what teenagers watch. Not like some people.' She snatched the DVD box away from him and put it down on the counter. 'Hey! Rav! Aren't you going to serve us?'

Ashley had a feeling he'd been trying to ignore them, but Vikki obviously knew him, and she wasn't going to let him get away with it. She reached over the counter and pulled at his sleeve. *'Rav!'*

He looked up and sighed. 'Come on, Vikki. You know I can't give you that. You're not eighteen.'

The Hyena nodded. 'That's right.' He looked at Ashley. 'You're better off without . . . without things like that.'

Vikki turned round and gave him a long, hostile stare. He grew even pinker, but he didn't back away. Instead, he looked straight past her, over the counter.

'You've . . . um . . . I know this sort of thing is awkward, Ravinder. Don't worry. I'll back you up.'

'Thank you, Mr Galt,' Ravinder said politely. But he didn't look overjoyed. 'I'll ask these young ladies to choose something else, shall I?'

The Hyena nodded and turned back to the racks. Vikki leaned on the counter and gave Ravinder a long, smouldering look. 'OK,' she murmured. 'I'll choose another one. I'll have . . . um . . . *this* one.'

Picking *Street Stalker* off the counter again, she held it out to him.

Ravinder pulled a face. 'Give us a break, Vik,' he muttered. He nodded towards the Hyena. 'You know what his mother's like. If she thinks we're not doing things right, there'll be all sorts of trouble.'

'What's the problem?' Vikki murmured. 'We're

with an adult, aren't we? Why don't you issue it to him?'

She glanced over her shoulder, at the Hyena's back, and Ravinder pinched his mouth shut, so that he wouldn't laugh.

'I can't do that.'

"Course you can.' Vikki picked up the pen. 'Look.' Reaching across the counter, she wrote the details herself, booking *Street Stalker* out to the Hyena. It was the last entry on the sheet, and she flipped the page over and held out her money. 'There you are. All done and dusted.'

Ravinder hesitated for a second. Then he gave in and found the DVD. As he slipped it into the box, he put a finger to his lips and Vikki grinned and wiggled her fingers in a little wave.

'Bye, Rav.' She tapped Ashley on the shoulder. 'Come on. Let's phone my mum and say I'm staying. If we get some pizzas, I can watch the DVD too.'

She bounded out of the shop, full of her new idea. Ashley was a little slower and, as she turned to follow, the Hyena moved away from the racks to stand in her way.

'I . . . um . . . ' He was very pink now, and breathing hard as he spoke. The words were causing him trouble. 'That young lady you're with . . . she's . . . um . . . I wouldn't like to see you get into trouble.'

Ashley stiffened. 'Why should I get into trouble?'

The Hyena took a breath. 'I mean she's a bit . . . if I were your father—'

'You're not my father,' Ashley said. 'My father's dead. And, for your information, Vikki is my best friend and she's really great. Excuse me, please.'

Pushing past him, she strode out of the shop. Vikki was on the pavement outside, grinning all over her face.

'I didn't know you'd got it in you.'

Ashley scowled. 'People keep treating me as if I haven't got a brain. Just because my mother's ill, it doesn't mean I'm a complete idiot. Let's go home and phone your mum.'

She stamped off down the road, without waiting for Vikki.

RAVINDER

That Vikki. She's a spoilt brat.

The business with the DVD was typical. She knew she was out of order, but she wasn't going to give in. Once Mr Galt interfered, that was it. She was determined to beat him.

She's the same with everyone. Even her boyfriend, Matt. Matt's sister, Ginger, is a mate of mine—ever since we were at school—and you ought to hear what she's got to say about Vikki. She hates her guts. Matt and Ginger are really close and he tells her everything. She goes ballistic about the way Vikki walks all over him.

That's Matt's lookout, I reckon, if he's stupid enough to go out with someone like that. But Vikki shouldn't pick on Mr Galt. He hasn't got a clue how to deal with a number like her.

He may be the original fogey, but he's got a good heart. When Kulvinder cut her leg, he shut up their shop so he could drive her to the hospital. And he didn't say a word about the blood on the upholstery, even though that car was his pride and joy.

That argument with Vikki must have shaken him up. When she went, he just stood and stared after her and her friend. Stared and stared, like an old man, for a good couple of minutes.

Next time Ginger comes in, I'm going to see if she can do something about it. If anyone can get Vikki to lay off Mr Galt, it'll be Ginger. She's great at handling people.

She'd be wonderful in the shop.

Pity she's going out with Phil Carson.

After all the fuss. *Street Stalker* turned out to be a really dreadful film. Even Vikki had to admit it. For most of the second half, she kept up a running commentary.

'And there's a dark corner! Is he going to jump out of there? Is he? Isn't he? AAAARGH! It's a cat. So now she's a nervous wreck. And of course he's going to come when she *doesn't* expect it. Maybe when she puts the key in the lock and opens the door. Or maybe in the kitchen—yes, it's going to be the kitchen—'

A face pressed itself flat against the kitchen window on the screen, and Vikki shrieked and buried her head in the cushions on the couch.

'Oh, I can't bear it! It's so dreadful! Rewind it, Ash, so we can see that bit again.'

Pauline was laughing too. Snatching the remote control out of Ashley's hand, she rewound the DVD and Vikki started again, in the same bright voice.

'And there's a dark corner! Is he going to jump out of there? Is he? Isn't he—?'

It was half-past nine by the time they finished the film and the pizzas. Vikki's father knocked on the door and she pulled a face.

'Aw, *Dad*! I could've walked home on my own.'

Her father was large and calm. He patted her on the head. 'Think I'm worried about *you*? It's the lads I'm thinking of. They don't stand much chance if they run into you on a dark night.'

'They'd be quite safe,' Vikki said demurely. 'Unless it was Eddie Beale, of course. Now if I was to meet him . . . ' She fluttered her eyelids like Minnie Mouse and looked meaningly at Ashley.

Her father hauled her out of the chair. 'If you met Eddie Beale, he'd stare straight over your head. He doesn't have anything to do with little girls. Now let's be having you. Some of us have to go to work in the morning.'

Vikki went, with a loud moan, and Pauline leaned back against her cushions, giggling weakly.

'She's a real hoot, isn't she? That's the best evening I've had for ages. It was really kind of Tricia to think of lending us the DVD player.'

Ashley opened her mouth. And shut it again.

'Homework?' Pauline said.

'I haven't got any. I did it in break.'

'That's good. Why don't we have some cocoa and do the crossword then?'

'You're not too tired?' Ashley said.

'I'm fine.' Pauline smiled. 'You know, I really think I'm getting a bit better.'

117

Ashley thought so too. She was humming as she went to make the cocoa.

It was Ashley who was tired. By the time they'd finished the crossword, she was so sleepy that she had to keep jerking herself awake.

'Help me on with my nightie,' Pauline said. 'Then you can go to bed.'

'But what about you?'

'I'll manage. I can sit up in bed and read. Go on. You're no use to me if you fall asleep down here.'

Ashley yawned. 'I'll just wash up the cups.'

'You will not. Why don't you stop *working*! I'll wash the cups tomorrow. It'll give me something to do.'

'OK,' Ashley said weakly.

She nearly said. *If I put your nightie on, can you brush your own hair?* But she knew the answer to that. It wasn't fair to ask. She went to fetch the hairbrush and the nightdress.

By the time she crawled up the stairs, she was utterly exhausted. She expected to fall fast asleep the moment her head hit the pillow, and she did.

But some time after midnight she woke up abruptly from her first, heavy sleep. Pauline was snoring downstairs, and the cistern in the bathroom was playing its usual monotonous tune, against a background of dull roaring from the traffic in the Row. Ashley twisted restlessly under her duvet, with every sound echoing in her head. The more she tried to ignore the little noises, the louder they sounded.

And then she heard a noise she couldn't place.

Scratch.

Her eyes flickered open.

Scratch-scratch.

It seemed to be coming from the back of the house. A harsh, scraping noise, like something sharp being drawn along a metal surface. Without switching the light on, Ashley climbed out of bed and padded into the bathroom.

Scratch.

The noise was coming from below, from somewhere close to the wall outside. For a moment, Ashley imagined silly things, like giant rats gnawing old saucepans. Then she pulled herself together and tried to visualize the things outside. What was made of metal?

Scratch-scratch-scratch.

Not the window-frame. That was wooden. And the walls were brick, covered with pebble-dash, and the windows were glass. There was nothing metal. The only other thing out there was the clothes-line which stretched from the pole in the garden right up to the house. Right up to—

Suddenly, she remembered. The clothes-line was tied on to the downpipe from the gutter. That was metal. Whatever was out there was scraping away at the downpipe.

Creeping over to the window, she peered down. Immediately, she saw that she was right about the downpipe. Someone was hunched at the bottom of it. A man.

Got you!

It was the man who'd sent the letters. It had to be! Ashley gave a small, triumphant grin in the dark. Then she crept back into her bedroom and found the torch in her chest of drawers.

When she went back into the bathroom, the scratching noise was still going on. She crouched by the window, working out exactly what she was going to do. When she was sure, she switched the torch on, jumped to her feet and flung the window open.

The man moved the moment the light hit him, covering his face with one arm and twisting away from her. She had a confused impression of a dark tracksuit with a hood pulled up to hide his face. Then he was scrambling over the fence, into Mrs Mac's garden.

He'll smash her pots, Ashley thought, as she followed him with the torch. *Mrs Mac'll be furious.*

But there was no sound of breaking. Whoever he

was, he knew how to move. Even though she leaned right out of the window, shining the torch across the back of the houses, she couldn't catch him again. He must be sneaking round the side of Mrs Mac's, heading for the street.

She wanted to race down the stairs and fling herself through the back door, so that she could follow him through the midnight streets and see where he went to ground. But she had enough sense not to start that. She didn't even go down to see what he had been doing with the downpipe. If she woke Pauline up, there would be questions.

She'd check it out in the morning.

SPIDER MO
Did I see him? 'Course I seen him. Fell over my head, didn't he?

Wasn't hurting no one. Just lying in that alley round the side of the house, to get out of the wind. And then—POW! A boot in the ear.

(I'm used to that. People don't notice me, see. When you sleep outside, you get to be Mrs Invisible.)

This one noticed me, though. He stopped beside me and I opened my eyes and saw—

Ha! Thought I was going to tell, didn't you?

I'm not stupid. The minute I clocked his face, I got the message. See me—and you'll be sorry. So I started rolling my eyes, as if I was right out of it. Then I slid over sideways, on top of all my bags.

(Got to take care of the bags. Some people'll steal anything. Had a scarf pinched right off my neck the other night.)

I lay on my bags, pretending I'd passed out. Hoping he was in too much of a hurry to kick my head in. He hung around for a couple of seconds, but I wasn't dumb enough to open my eyes. I stayed curled round the bags, like a dead hedgehog, and at last he took himself off.

So I didn't see anything. OK? Not a whisker. That's how I've lasted so long. I don't see things.

Nothing.

13

It was him. The same man.

The moment Ashley looked at the downpipe next morning, and saw the scratches, she knew for sure. There was a single word gouged on to the downpipe, in letters that went right through the black paint.

CINDY.

Underneath it there was a shape, a perfect drop. Like a drop of blood.

He'd crouched under her window and scratched it, right outside the kitchen door. Ashley could see his footprints in the loose earth. The ground was churned and trampled round the pipe, but there were two or three clear prints further along, the marks of heavy shoes, with a deep tread. They were in the flowerbed beside the fence, where he'd come through from Mrs Mac's.

He'd come through and crouched there in the cold, under her window. Scratching the five letters that meant, *I know who you are. I can give you away.*

What else would he have done if she hadn't disturbed him? What did the drop of blood mean?

For the first time, she began to feel afraid.

'What did he scratch?' Vikki said.

They were sitting in the library, pretending to work on the computers. Ashley reached over and tapped out the word on the keyboard, to avoid saying it out loud. It appeared in the *Search* box.

Cindy.

Vikki bit her lip. 'He knew? It must be the same person, mustn't it?'

'Suppose so.' Ashley frowned. 'But why? What's the point?'

'He's trying to scare you,' Vikki said. She ran the mouse backwards and forwards on the mat, not looking at Ashley. '*Are* you scared?'

'What of?' Ashley said lightly. 'A few scratches on the paint?'

'It's not what he did,' Vikki muttered. 'It's what he *might* do.'

Ashley wasn't going to admit that she'd thought of that as well. 'Oh, wow!' she said sarcastically. 'You mean—he might scratch on the back door next? That *would* be scary.'

Vikki kicked her under the table. 'Don't pretend you're not worried. You know I can tell. D'you want me to send Matt round tonight? To keep an eye open?'

'And make more footprints in the flowerbeds?'

'Footprints?' Vikki sat bolt upright and her fingers

tapped the word on to the keyboard. *Footprints.* 'You didn't say that before. If there's footprints, you've got him! All you've got to do is go home and take a plaster cast. Then we can go to see Eddie.'

That was just like Vikki. Listening was never enough for her. She always had to be doing something. Ashley sighed.

'Eddie's not going to care about scratches on a drainpipe.'

'Of course he is. It was a *midnight intruder*!' Vikki was sitting on the very edge of her chair now. 'You've got to find out who it was. I'll come round straight after school and we'll do a plaster cast—'

'Don't be silly. We haven't got any plaster.'

Vikki waved the objection away. 'We'll measure the footprints and do a drawing, then. And take it round to Eddie and—'

Ashley saw Mrs Hunt coming into the library, and she nudged Vikki hard. Without hesitation, Vikki clicked on *Search*, smiling cherubically.

But the computer was too quick for her. By the time Mrs Hunt reached them, the answer was on the screen.

No match for Cindy Footprints

'Working hard?' Mrs Hunt said. She looked at the screen and smiled acidly. 'It looks as though you need a bit more practise.' The smile snapped off her face. 'I think you'd better stay after school and memorize the rules for working on the computers.'

Vikki went pink. 'But, Mrs Hunt! We've got something really important to do this afternoon. And anyway, Ash has to get home and look after her mother—'

'Then she shouldn't have been wasting her time in school. These computers aren't toys.' Mrs Hunt's face was spiteful now. 'I'm sure Ashley's mother won't fade away just because she's half an hour later coming home.'

Vikki was all set to argue. 'But you don't understand! Ashley's mother is—'

Ashley kicked her under the table and she stopped, but she was still furious. The moment Mrs Hunt disappeared, she typed *Smelly Hunt* into the computer.

'I bet there are hundreds of matches for that,' she said.

When they came out of school at last, Joe was by the gate. He grinned at Ashley and fell into step.

'What are you doing here?' Vikki scowled at him. She wasn't one for forgiving and forgetting.

Joe ignored her, and answered as though Ashley

had asked the question. 'Eddie asked what you were up to. I didn't know, so I came to find out.'

'I've been doing a detention,' Ashley said. She went on walking briskly down the road. She wasn't sure she could cope with Joe at the moment.

Vikki ran after her. 'Don't be stupid! This is your chance. You can send Eddie a message!'

Joe came up on the other side. 'You want me to tell Eddie something?'

'No I don't,' Ashley said crossly.

Joe's eyes were glittering like chips of coal in his pale face. 'Something's happened, hasn't it?'

'Of course not!' Ashley hoisted her bag higher on one shoulder, like a barrier, and walked away, but Vikki trotted along beside her, refusing to be shaken off.

'You idiot!' she hissed. 'What's the matter? Do you *like* being stalked?'

'I'm not being stalked!'

'Yes you are. That's what it is. *Stalking.* You've got to get Eddie to help.'

'But I don't even know him.'

'Of course you do. He sent you that DVD player.' Vikki caught hold of Ashley's sleeve, dragging her to a standstill as Joe came up behind them.

He wasn't hurrying. He was slouching along, mumbling under his breath. As he came closer, Ashley could hear the words and he wasn't saying them in his own voice.

' . . . don't need any help,' he was muttering. ' . . . just got to concentrate . . . I'll be fine . . . I can manage . . . '

One of his shoulders was lifted higher than the other, and his face was closed and inaccessible. Frowning.

' . . . can't ask for help . . . got to keep going . . . '

Vikki suddenly gave a loud giggle.

'What's up with you?' Ashley said. She was annoyed that she couldn't see the joke.

Vikki started laughing, but Joe didn't even glance at her. He just went on muttering.

' . . . perfectly all right . . . got to be perfect . . . I can cope . . . '

'I don't see—' Ashley began.

And then, suddenly, horribly, she did see. It was like the sort of trick picture that shifts from non sense to sense as you stare at it. One moment Joe looked completely mad, and the next she saw— herself. Scurrying along with her face turned away from everyone else. Fooling herself that she could manage.

She went bright red. 'Stop it!'

' . . . can't let anyone help . . . ' Joe mumbled.

'Stop it!' Ashley shouted.

She began to run away, racing between the blocks of flats and round Toronto House into the cinema car park. When she came out on to the Row, the traffic lights were in her favour and she went straight across.

She thought she'd shaken the others off, but as she turned to walk along the Row, Joe appeared at her elbow.

'Hi,' he said.

'Go away,' Ashley growled. She looked behind, expecting to see Vikki.

'It's all right,' Joe said. 'I told her to beat it. I said Eddie wouldn't listen to you unless you were on your own.'

I'm not going to tell Eddie! Ashley wanted to say. *I can handle it.* But she remembered how Joe had looked. How he'd said those words. *I can manage.* Shabby and scuttling. Pathetic.

'My . . . mum doesn't know,' she said slowly. 'About any of this.'

'So?' Joe shrugged. 'Who's going to tell her?' He looked sideways at Ashley. 'Come on. Spit it out.'

They were outside Fat Annie's when Ashley knew she was going to tell him. She was on the verge of speaking when she felt someone watching her. Glancing round, she saw Mrs Hunt inside the shop, staring through the window. Behind her was the Hyena.

He was staring too.

Ashley began to walk faster. 'Let's get round the corner. Then I'll tell you.'

'OK,' Joe said again. 'Hang on a minute, though.'

He stopped and turned to face the window. Pulling a face, he stuck his tongue out at Mrs Hunt, as far as it would go.

Then he followed Ashley into Railway Street.

SHEILA HUNT
Well!

Other teachers tell me that they are often subjected to that type of insolence, but I will not tolerate rude behaviour, so when the boy stuck his tongue out, I was speechless for a moment.

Then I pulled myself together and rapped on the counter. Mr Galt was goggling out of the window like a man struck deaf and dumb.

'If you don't mind!' I said.

He dragged his eyes back to my shopping. But even while he was weighing my tomatoes I saw him sneaking glances through the window.

'Something wrong?' I said sharply.

He coloured. 'I . . . er . . . I'm sorry, Mrs Hunt. I was taken aback. Seeing Ashley with that boy—'

I couldn't help feeling sorry for him. He's just the sort of man who would be taken in by Ashley. Those big blue eyes of hers, and that oh-so-innocent look.

'You would be surprised,' I said, 'by some of the company Ashley Putnam keeps. Her best friend is a most undesirable girl. Most undesirable. That boy is respectable by comparison, even if his manners are atrocious. Maybe he's her brother.'

'Oh no!' For some reason, Mr Galt looked ridiculously shocked. 'There's no brother. She … um … she hasn't got anyone. She … she lives with her mother, and that's why—'

'Thank you.' I cut him off. It's not my habit to gossip about my pupils.

Ashley Putnam used to be a promising girl. Very bright and hardworking, and a good gymnast, too. But it's obviously the usual story. She's discovered boys and work's gone out of the window.

Children today are so lazy.

14

Ashley slid her key into the lock. 'Remember,' she said. 'You mustn't tell my mum. Not a word.'

'No worries,' Joe said as he walked in after her.

There was a faint, unfamiliar scent in the hall. Like bluebells, or hyacinths. Ashley frowned, trying to work out what it was, but Joe knew straight away.

'Tricia's been.' He grinned and walked into the front room. 'Hi, Pauline,' he said. And then, 'You're looking good. I like the hair.'

'What hair?' Ashley hurried after him.

Pauline was sitting at the table peeling sprouts. She looked cheerful and excited—and different. Her great mass of hair had vanished. Someone had cut it into smart wisps at the front and chopped it as short as Joe's at the back. The bones of her face looked stronger and more solid as she grinned up at them both.

'Do you like it? Tricia did it.'

'I—' Ashley felt so strange that she had to sit down.

Pauline's smile faltered. 'You don't like it?'

'It's not that—'

'Of course it's not,' Joe said firmly. 'It's great. Come on. Ash. You've got to admit it.'

He was right. It looked wonderful. Ashley couldn't understand why she felt angry. She forced a smile on to her face.

'It's beautiful. It was just a shock, that's all. You look about ten years younger.'

Pauline grinned. 'Only ten? Tricia said fifteen. She was round for coffee, and suddenly she said, *Honestly, Paul, you'd look fifteen years younger with all that hair off. And it would be much more practical, too. Why don't I go home and get my scissors?* And she did. Just like that. Didn't she do it well?'

'It's brilliant,' Ashley said, fighting the ugly, angry lump in her throat.

Joe grinned. 'Tricia's a genius with scissors. She even does Sam's hair, and you've got to be good to make something look as ragged as that.'

'Sam?' Pauline leaned forward. 'Has she got ragged hair? I thought she was a model?'

'I'm not A Model!' Joe flung himself on to a chair, straddling it backwards with his legs stretched out. His voice was shrill and he tilted his chin aggressively. 'I do some modelling, but that's not all I'm good for. Why do you want to put me in a box?' He ran his fingers through his hair, leaving it standing on end, and for a moment Ashley could have sworn it was blonde.

Pauline was giggling. Joe jumped to his feet and glared at her.

'You think that's funny?' He tossed his head. 'You're *pathetic*!'

Still being Sam, he strutted out to the kitchen as though his legs were twice as long, and Pauline laughed out loud, shaking her head at Ashley. 'How does he do it?'

Ashley didn't answer. She heard a rattle as Joe picked up the matchbox in the kitchen, and she remembered Sam, in the warehouse.

Fire.

'I—Hang on, Mum. I'll make a drink.'

She shot down the hall. Joe was standing in the kitchen with a lighted match in his hand and his head tilted back. He was lowering the flame towards his open mouth and for one crazy moment Ashley saw him lit up red and gold. Playing with danger. She froze, waiting for a tongue of fire to shoot across the kitchen.

Then Joe laughed and blew out the match.

'You lunatic!' Ashley said. 'You could've—'

'Don't be silly.' Joe grinned at her, mockingly. 'It was only a match. Are we going in the garden?'

Ashley blinked, and the world shrank back to normal. He was right, of course. The little match flame had been real, but all the rest—the fire and the danger and the drama—were imaginary. He'd tricked her into seeing them. A match was only a match.

And a scratch was only a scratch.

She pushed the back door open, abruptly. 'Come on then.'

Joe didn't waste time on the winter grass and the spindly bushes. Slipping through the door, he crouched beside the downpipe, examining the letters. With one forefinger, he traced out their shapes in the air. C.I.N.D.Y.

'Why that name?' he said.

'He's gloating. Letting me know he's found out—'

'I know *that*. I mean—why do you use that tag?'

Ashley looked down at her feet. 'No reason,' she said gruffly.

Joe raised one eyebrow, but he didn't push it. Turning sideways, he studied the footprints in the flowerbed. 'I think I'll draw these. Have you got a bit of paper?'

Ashley fetched him a pencil and paper from the kitchen. Then she went inside to make the tea, in case Pauline wondered what they were doing.

When she came out again, Joe had drawn two footprints, and he was checking the pattern, to make sure he'd got it exactly right.

'Want me to take this to Eddie?' he said.

Ashley frowned down at the pattern of waves and dots he had drawn. Three curves to each wave. Four waves on the sole and two on the heel. Six dots in between the front waves, and four nearer the back. Size ten or eleven at least. 'What can Eddie do?' she said.

Joe looked. 'You don't understand about him, do you?'

'No I don't.' Ashley was starting to find it rather annoying. 'Why does everyone keep going on about him?'

'Because he's the boss. He knows everyone, and people do what he says.'

'So why would he take any notice of me?'

Joe shrugged. 'Dunno, but he seems to. Maybe he's got a soft spot for cartwheels. He likes a show.'

'But he sent me a DVD player for that. We're all square.'

'A DVD player?, Joe looked amused. 'You think that's all he's done? Given you a DVD player?'

Ashley frowned, not understanding. 'What else?'

'Oh, come on!' Joe jerked his head towards the house. 'Why d'you think Tricia came round? She's very nice, but she'd never do something like that on her own.'

'You mean—Eddie sent her? Why would he do that?'

Joe squatted back on his heels. 'Because he wants to help you. He asked about you, after the party. *What's she like, that girl? What kind of life does she have?*'

'And you . . . said . . . ?' Ashley could hardly get the words out.

Joe shrugged. 'I said you spend your life looking after your mum. And she's really nice—but she's bored out of her mind. Needs a bit of company. *I reckon her mother could do with a friend,* I said.'

'So it's all fake?'

'Don't be so stupid!' Joe stood up. 'Tricia really likes her. Tricia likes everyone. But she'd never have thought of coming round if Eddie hadn't suggested—'

Ashley clenched her fists. 'He didn't have to.'

'Of course he didn't have to! He did it to help. But you won't let anyone help, will you?' Suddenly, Joe was angry. He stood up and pushed his drawing of the footprint into Ashley's hand. 'Do what you want! No one's going to force you!'

He stamped into the house. Ashley heard him say goodbye to her mother and a moment later the front door slammed. Slowly, she unfolded the paper and looked down at it. Was Joe right? Should she ask Eddie for help?

No, it was ridiculous!

Pushing the paper into her pocket, she opened the kitchen door. She was about to step through when she heard her mother's voice.

'You won't know me next time you come!'

She was on the telephone. Ashley walked down

the hall and looked into the front room. Pauline was perched on the end of the bed, with the phone to her ear, and she was talking excitedly. Her whole face seemed to have come alive, in a way that Ashley had never seen before.

KAREN

I couldn't believe it when I picked up the phone and it was MUM! She hardly ever telephones us.

Janet thinks that's really mean, but I don't see what all the fuss is about. It's great when we go and see Mum—she's a real laugh—but there's nothing much to talk about on the phone.

So when she said, 'Hallo. That's Karen, isn't it?' I just said, 'Hi, Mum, I'll get Janet.'

I could see Louise frowning at me, because she wanted to talk to Mum, but she's always trying to make out Mum likes her best, so I was going to yell for Janet when Mum said, 'Hey, not so fast, I've got a surprise.'

She sounded quite different from usual—sort of bouncy. And then she told me, and I was so surprised that I yelled right in her ear.

'YOU'VE HAD YOUR HAIR CUT OFF??!!!'

That did it, of course. Louise crowded in, squeaking, 'Oh, you haven't spoilt it, have you?' and 'Did you keep the hair for us?' And Janet came rattling down the stairs because she'd heard something was up. And all the time, I'm yelling into the phone, 'Does it look good? When can we come and see it? Can we come and see you this weekend?' And Mum's laughing and laughing—

I can't wait to see her on Saturday.

139

15

The haircut was only the beginning. After that, Tricia seemed to be there every day.

On Wednesday, Ashley came home from school, worrying about what the stalker might have left, and discovered Pauline and Tricia playing Scrabble. They were giggling hysterically. Tricia grinned at her and waved a hand.

'I did a bit of shopping for you. While I had the car out.'

There was enough food for the rest of the week, and she laughed out loud when Ashley tried to pay for it.

'Don't be daft. It's only a few bits.'

There was nothing from the stalker on Thursday, either. But Pauline and Tricia were in the kitchen, with a chocolate cake cooling on the table.

'I thought I might as well do something useful,' Pauline said. 'While we were talking.'

Ashley stared at the cake and tried to remember the last one her mother had made. Four years ago? Five?

On Friday, Tricia was there again, with a bag of clothes and a message from Sam. *(She's finished with these, and would they fit Ashley?)* On Saturday she brought some leggings for Pauline, and on Sunday she walked in with a new sink plug, because the old one was leaking.

On Monday morning, Ashley opened the bathroom window while she was cleaning her teeth, and saw the autumn colours in the back garden. She went downstairs humming to herself. She felt wonderful.

'Hi, Mum. What do you fancy wearing today?'

Pauline was sitting on the edge of the bed, wriggling her feet into a pair of slippers. She grinned. 'How about those new black leggings? And my big orange jumper?'

'Great! You'll match the autumn leaves. They're amazing this year. You should see the trees round the school field. I'll just make the tea, and then I'll get your jumper.'

Still humming, Ashley went out to the kitchen. She put the kettle on, took the bread out of the bread bin, opened the curtains and—

No.

She froze. Her fingers clenched on the curtain, screwing the material tight.

From the other side of the window, a skull leered back with ugly, open eye sockets. Not a human skull, but a long, grotesque head, with twisting horns, jammed sideways on to the sill. Two long bones were propped at the sides, meeting over the top in an arch,

141

and someone had scrawled ugly, irregular letters across the white dome of the skull.

CINDY . . . TROUBLE . . .

The words were written in felt pen, in staring purple capitals. Above them, the ends of the bones lay round and smooth against the glass. Someone had fixed them on to the windowsill with big clots of Blu-Tack.

It took Ashley a moment to realize that she was looking at a sheep's skull, and even recognizing it didn't dull the shock. Because it wasn't the skull itself that was horrible. It was the thought of *him*. His thick, pale fingers scrabbling about in the dark, crawling over the kitchen window and squashing the Blu-Tack into place. She didn't know what he looked like, but she could imagine those fingers, as clearly as she could see the bones.

I can't, she thought. *I can't touch them.*

Then her mother called from the front room. 'Ash? You'll be late if you don't keep moving.'

And she knew that she could do it after all. She had to do it, before Pauline saw. Grabbing a wet rag from under the sink, she called back.

'There's some . . . er . . . bird's mess on the window. I'm just going out to wipe it off.'

'You haven't got time—'

'Of course I have. Anyway, I can't leave it. It's disgusting.'

Ashley slipped out of the back door. The moment she was outside, she saw that there were more footprints in the damp earth. They were even clearer than yesterday's. A pattern of waves and dots, with three curves to each wave. Four waves on the sole and two on the heel. Six dots in between the front waves, and four nearer the back.

That was his tag. As recognizable as her own. It was the same man all the time.

Reaching across the flowerbed, to avoid smudging the footprints, she pulled the skull free and laid it down on the path. Then she pulled off the long bones and the Blu-Tack, and looked round for a place to hide them.

'Ashley! Hurry up!' Pauline was getting anxious.

Quickly, Ashley tucked the bones and the skull behind the dustbin. Then, with a last look at the footprints, she whisked back into the kitchen.

'You didn't have to do that,' Pauline called. 'I could have managed.'

'Oh sure. It would only have taken you all day.' Ashley rubbed both hands fiercely under the hot tap, getting rid of the feel of the bones. 'It's all right. Don't fuss.'

'But you haven't got much time left. Let me do something.'

Ashley heard the shuffle of sticks as her mother

started walking across the room. It looked as though she was having another good day. Lucky the bones were out of sight.

Pauline appeared in the kitchen and collapsed on to a chair. She was out of breath, but she was grinning.

'I can get dressed myself if you'll bring the clothes down,' she said.

'Are you sure?'

'I think so. You have some breakfast.'

Ashley had never felt less like eating, but she gulped down a couple of Weetabix and raced upstairs for the leggings and the jumper.

She was struggling not to think about the bones. They were safely tucked away behind the dustbin. What was the point of worrying about them? A match was only a match. A scratch was only a scratch. And a bone was only a bone.

She was still trying to convince herself as she walked up the road to school. Nothing serious had happened. *A letter is only a piece of paper. A word on a drainpipe is only a scratch. A sheep's skull is just a piece of bone.* Nothing to get hung up on.

As long as her mother didn't decide to look behind the dustbin.

* * *

That danger nagged away at her, all day. She couldn't wait to get home, and the last lesson in the afternoon seemed to drag on for ever. Mr Neale was dictating History notes and when the bell rang he hadn't quite finished. Some people stood up and he banged on his desk.

'How about some manners?'

'Aw, sir!' There were moans from the people who had buses to catch, but he wouldn't relent. So when he finally did let them go, they all charged for the door at once. Ashley and Vikki had to wait to get out of the classroom.

'Silly idiots.' Vikki took out her nail varnish. 'What's the big hurry? It's only another two or three minutes.' She started painting her left thumbnail black. 'What d'you reckon. Ash? Would it look nice with those little gold stars stuck on it?'

Ashley tried to focus her mind on thumbnails. 'Maybe. Only one, though. Off centre.'

Vikki started on the right hand nail. She didn't look up, but she said, 'You OK, Ash? You look a bit hassled.'

'I'm fine,' Ashley said quickly. 'Just want to get home, that's all.'

· 'Has something else happened?' Vikki did look up then. Sharply, to catch her off guard. But Ashley was ready. Her face and her voice were both perfectly calm.

'Everything's fine.'

At that moment, the doorway cleared. Vikki began to screw the lid back on to her nail varnish bottle, but Ashley didn't wait for her. She headed straight for home.

When she arrived, there were no lights on. That was unusual. It wasn't completely dark, but it must be pretty dim in there, and her mother never sat in the dark unless she fell asleep. Or unless—

Ashley unlocked the door quickly and threw it open. 'Mum?'

There was no answer.

Her heart gave an enormous leap. That was what she always dreaded. She ran into the front room and switched on the light. But she didn't see what she was afraid of. Her mother wasn't lying there, sprawled helpless on the floor. She wasn't there at all.

The room was empty.

That was so extraordinary that for a second Ashley's mind went blank. Then she saw the note lying on the table.

> *Dear Ashie, Tricia and her friend Phil came in a car.*
> *We've gone to the country to see the autumn leaves.*
> *Back soon. Love, Mum.*

Pauline had gone out in a car? That hadn't happened since the twins grew so big that they couldn't all fit into Frank and Janet's Metro. Ashley had begun to think she'd never go out again.

But she had—and it was brilliant timing. The perfect opportunity to get rid of the skull.

Going through the kitchen, Ashley snatched a couple of plastic carrier bags out of the drawer. Then she went outside and crouched down beside the dustbin, feeling round the back for the skull.

Her fingers met the jagged edges of broken bone.

She snatched her hand back and pulled the dustbin away. The skull lay exactly where she left it, but someone had smashed the top in. With a boot maybe, or a hammer.

Behind it, lying across the bones, was a brown envelope, with a word written across it in the same purple felt pen that had scrawled on the skull.

CINDY.

Ashley bent down and picked it up. She felt completely unemotional. Icy-calm. But when she looked down at her arm, she saw that it was shaking. *How strange. I must be afraid after all.* Slowly, she opened the top of the envelope.

It was full of photographs. There were half a dozen of them and they were all pictures of her.

There she was, walking past the chippie. Standing

by the DVD shop. Waiting to cross at the traffic lights. Talking to Vikki on the corner of Railway Street. The angles were different, but the pictures were all variations on a theme. In every one, she was somewhere in the Row, not looking straight at the camera but busy with her own life. And there was another thing that they had in common as well.

Someone had drawn on each one, in felt pen. A jagged black line running from top to bottom.

Right through her head.

With a huge effort, Ashley turned the pictures over. Five of them were blank on the back. The sixth said, *You're going to get into trouble . . .*

Just as she thought she was going to scream, she heard the car draw up outside.

PHIL
When Eddie asks you to do something, you don't exactly argue. I mean—he's the boss, isn't he? Like, there was ten or eleven of us in the pub on Thursday night, and he comes in and says, 'I need a driver for tomorrow. Got to be someone with a clean licence. I don't want any hassle.'

That knocked three of them out straight away, of course, but there were plenty of other blokes. I didn't even look up from my beer.

But Eddie seems to have taken to me recently. He clapped me on the back. 'Tricia wants to go out for a drive, with a friend of hers. Fancy being the chauffeur?'

I don't like to tell you what the others said. But they were wrong. When I get to Tricia's, it turns out we're doing a good deed. It's Ashley Putnam's mum who's going for a ride. Pauline, from Railway Street.

It looked like a dull day, especially when we picked up Pauline and she and Tricia piled into the back together. I thought, Eddie wasn't joking when he said I was going to be a chauffeur.

How wrong can you be?

We went out into the country, to look at the autumn leaves, and we were in fits, all the way. The two of them seemed to set each other off, and as for jokes—well, I'm not going to repeat the jokes they told, but I had to stop the car twice, I was laughing so much. Ginger's told me lots about that family, but she never told me Ashley's mum was so funny.

She was pretty wiped out by the time we got back, though. Even Tricia stopped talking and let her alone. 'We'll just drop Pauline off,' she said. 'OK, Phil? We won't go in.'

That was the plan. But the moment the car pulls up, Ashley—Pauline's daughter—shoots out of the house, like a bomb. And it's not her mum she wants to talk to.

It's Tricia. She knocked on the window and beckoned, and when Tricia got out she pulled her away from the car and started whispering.

'What's that?' Pauline says. 'What's going on?'

But she's not asking very hard, because she's so tired. And I wasn't going to ask either. I've only been with Eddie a year or so, but that's one thing I've learnt. Keep your nose out of things.

After five minutes or so, Tricia came over and asked me to carry Pauline inside. I picked her up—there's no weight to her at all—took her inside and put her down on the bed. She looked ready to sleep for a week.

Tricia was right behind me. 'Take care of yourself,' she said, and she patted Pauline's hand. 'I'll be round soon.'

Then we took ourselves off. I thought Tricia might have explained the whispering, but she didn't say a word.

All she said was, 'Come back to my place. We haven't got long. I need the car here again at midnight.'

I gave her a funny look. Like, Who d'you think you are, giving me orders? But she didn't turn a hair.

'Eddie's business,' she said. 'Ashley wants to see him. We're picking her up as soon as Pauline's asleep.'

16

Ashley lay on her bed, waiting for midnight and going over what Tricia had said, again and again.

Eddie might help you. But it's not automatic. People are always after him for things. You'll have to get his attention.

How was she going to do that? Go in and yell at him? Wear something dramatic? (That was a laugh, given her wardrobe.) Set fire to his hair?

Round and round went her mind, growing wilder and wilder. And all the time, she knew that there was only one thing she could really try. Only one thing she could do well enough.

Her turn. Her trick.

Tricia and Phil were there at midnight, exactly as Tricia had promised. Ashley crept out of the alley, stepping over Spider Mo, and slid into the car.

'Here we go, then,' Tricia said, as the car pulled away. 'It's not easy, tracking Eddie down, but we'll give it a whirl. He and Sam have got a thing about this new club at the moment. Nightrap. They're usually there a couple of times a week, so we'll try that. Have you brought the things?'

Ashley passed the bag forward for her to see the shattered skull and the letters and the photographs. Tricia rummaged through them, holding the photographs up to the window to catch the light. When she saw the jagged, scrawled lines, she shuddered.

'He's a nasty piece of work, isn't he? Deserves a good long talk with Eddie.'

'You think there's a chance Eddie's going to be interested?'

'Maybe.' Tricia shrugged and passed the bag back. 'It's worth a go. Depends if something else has cropped up. If not, he might be looking for an entertainment.'

Ashley twisted the top of the bag tightly, trying to think of it all like that. An entertainment. A show. What she had to do was put on a better show than anyone else. She could feel her blood flowing faster as her body prepared for it.

'Suppose they won't let me into the club?'

Tricia shook her head. 'No problem.'

Ashley didn't really believe it, but she hadn't seen Eddie's name in action. When the doorman raised his eyebrows at her, Tricia just muttered at him.

'Come to see Eddie.'

That was enough. He winked and waved them through to the stairs.

They went down into smoky darkness, hearing

feet thud over their heads as they walked under the balcony. The disco lights lit up crowds of people on the main dance floor, and more people above them, all dancing fast and frantically. There was a circular balcony, running all the way round the club and everywhere—in front, behind, left and right and above—there were moving bodies, pulsing in time to the music. It was like stepping into a cauldron boiling with energy.

Ashley couldn't imagine how they were going to find anyone, but Tricia leaned closer, bellowing into her ear.

'See Eddie? Up on the balcony.'

Ashley looked across the club, to the steps that led up to the balcony. And the one still point. At the top of the steps, just to one side, was a table with people sitting round it.

Ashley could see why Eddie chose to be there. The table was half hidden, but it dominated the whole place. From there, he could see everything that was going on.

Sam was leaning over the wrought-iron balustrade, looking at the dancers. Her dress caught the lights, glittering red, then purple, then silver. Beside her, perched on the broad rail, was Doug, talking to a couple of other men.

Eddie was slightly further back than the others,

with his chair tilted and a glass in his hand. It was impossible to make out his expression, but he was watching what was going on below.

Tricia put her mouth right against Ashley's ear. 'We can't fight our way through this lot. Better wait for a break in the music.'

Ashley nodded. She didn't attempt to shout back. She was busy looking round the club, working out how to do what she wanted. There would only be a few seconds to get it right. No time to hesitate. The plan had to be clear in her head.

It was like getting ready to do a wall. She could feel her adrenalin level rising as she waited for the moment when the music stopped. That split second of almost-quiet before the voices rose. Pushing her carrier bag at Tricia, she cupped her hands round her mouth, to be ready.

And when the moment came, she yelled at the top of her voice.

'Stand back!'

It was the risk she'd taken at the party, but magnified a hundred times. She hardly believed the floor would clear for her. But it was as though people had been expecting something to happen. When she flung herself into the first cartwheel, they scattered in front of her, squeezing back from the centre of the floor.

She spun between them, over and over, right to the bottom of the stairs. Then she flipped over into a handstand and began to climb the stairs. She knew she could probably manage six steps, but she played safe and let her legs drop over after five, climbing the rest of the flight in a backbend.

As she went, the lights came up gradually. The whole club was silent, and she could feel the eyes on her back, but she wouldn't let herself think about them. She concentrated on climbing, and all she could see was the blue carpet on the stairs, inches away from her eyes.

Then, suddenly, there were no more stairs. She was at the top, and instead of staring at carpet, she was staring down at a pair of heavy black toecaps. They were polished to such a shine that she could see her face in them, and she knew, without being told, whose boots they were.

Sidling round them, she flipped the right way up, and turned towards Eddie. Very slowly, he tapped three fingers against the palm of his other hand, applauding. Mockingly. Watching her face.

Was that good or bad? What was she supposed to do? Ashley looked round at the others—Sam and Doug, two heavies, and a couple of girls dressed to kill. Was it time for her to speak now? They were all listening, but she wasn't sure.

Then a voice came from under the table. A shrill, whining noise, like the voice of a bored child.

'That's *nothing*. I could do that when I was *seven*. She's not expecting us to *clap*, is she?'

It was Joe.

Eddie's fingers stopped tapping and lay still in the palm of his hand. Everyone was quiet, waiting to see what would happen. She hadn't done enough yet. That was what Joe had been telling her.

So . . . what?

She glanced quickly over her shoulder, wondering whether she could make it down the stairs again. When she looked back, Eddie was staring. Cool and amused.

'Dull!' he said.

His eyes went sideways to the balcony rail, and her stomach clenched abruptly, as she understood what he wanted. She looked along the rail and thought of the danger. Then she looked back at him.

Quickly, before she could think, she spread her arms to the audience below, bowing left and right. Then—ignoring the half-hearted applause—she took three quick steps up. On to a chair. On to the table. And up on to the rail round the balcony. As fast as she could, not giving herself time to think, she went over into a handstand.

And she heard everyone gasp.

GINGER

You could have pushed me over with a banana.

It was Ashley Putnam.

(She's a friend of Vikki's and Matt reckons she does those fantastic graffitis. I used to reckon Vikki was kidding him about that, but now—well, see what you think.)

I was down on the floor, all on my own, in a flaming temper. Phil had promised to take me to Nightrap. Been promising for weeks. And then, at the last moment, there was a phone call: We'll have to meet there. And I can't make it till after twelve.

Was I pleased? You know the answer to that! I was just waiting for him to turn up so I could spit in his face and punch his nose sideways. And I knew just what I was going to yell while I did it.

It was a good night for a bit of drama. Eddie Beale was sitting up on the balcony, and the whole club had that feel you get when he's around. Like, something's going to happen. *And I tell you, I thought I was going to be the show. Me and Phil.*

But then Ashley turned up, out of nowhere.

She went cartwheeling across the floor, and strutting up the steps on her hands and suddenly I found I was one of the audience, after all. I was standing there gawping with everyone else.

Feeling the danger in the air.

When Ashley went up on the balcony rail, everyone edged into the middle of the floor. Partly to see better and partly to stay out of trouble. We all thought she was going to run round the rail, and we didn't want to be underneath if she fell off.

But she didn't run. She went over into a handstand.

Holy soap! You could have heard an ant sneeze. None of us could believe it. And when she started moving, I grabbed at the person next to me, like we were drowning. I was terrified to think—in case my brain made too much noise.

Left.

Right.

Left.

Right.

Every time Ashley moved an arm, I nearly died. But I couldn't have looked away. Not for a million pounds. I had to watch it all. Every lurch as she shifted her weight forward. Every wobble of her legs. And all the time, there's this voice going on in my head. She's nearly done a quarter. . . now it's a third of the way round . . . now it's almost half . . .

And then, when she was halfway round, she missed her grip. Her fingers slipped on the rail and I thought she was going right over.

I gasped. We all gasped. You just can't help yourself

when it's like that. Phil appeared out of nowhere and put his arm round me, but I hardly even noticed him. I was watching Ashley struggle to keep her balance. And my fingernails were digging into the palms of my hands.

Phil was the same. I could feel him holding his breath as she steadied herself and started off again. It's step by step, and you can't think of anything, except how can she go on, how can she have the strength? But she keeps going on. And on and on, until it's only another two or three hand-steps. Another one.

And then she's there.

She flipped off the rail and landed on the balcony, on her feet, and the place exploded. But she wasn't the one who needed the clapping. We needed it, to let the tension go. We needed to stamp and cheer and clap our hands raw to let out the energy and the fear and the frenzy of it.

Ashley didn't take any notice of the clapping. She just stood in front of Eddie, looking him straight in the eye. As if she was saying, OK now what are you going to do about it?

17

It was as if there was nobody else in the club. Only Eddie. Ashley stood in front of him, shaking slightly, and met his eyes square on.

'I need help,' she said. 'And you told me you always pay for good performances.'

Eddie nodded once, but he didn't smile. 'So what kind of help do you want?'

Ashley hadn't planned what she was going to say. And before she could think, Tricia came running across the club with the carrier bag in her hand. As the lights went down again, she came up the balcony steps.

Ashley grabbed the bag from her and turned it upside down over the table. 'Look!' she said fiercely. Bones fell helter skelter, mixed with photographs and pieces of paper. 'Look at those! How would you like to get messages like that?'

They were in a circle round the table now. Eddie and Sam, Tricia and Doug. Sam picked up the skull and ran her finger round the jagged hole in the top.

'Someone sent you *this?*'

Her face twisted in disgust. She dropped the skull back on to the table and rubbed at her hands.

'Doesn't look too good, does it?' said Doug. 'Whoever sent these, I wouldn't talk to him on your own, love.'

'But *why* send them?' Tricia spread out the photographs and looked down at them, wonderingly. 'Who hates you that much, Ashley?'

'Maybe he doesn't hate her,' Eddie said softly. 'Maybe he loves her.'

That's rubbish! Ashley wanted to say. *Don't talk rubbish!* But she could feel the others shifting uncomfortably around her. The skull leered up, threatening her in a different way, and the letters trembled on the table as the dancers round them stirred the air.

'Haven't you got any idea who sent them?' Tricia said.

'What about the shoes?' said a dark, sepulchral voice from Joe, still under the table.

Ashley remembered the drawings and took them out of her pocket. 'These are his shoes. I know they are. If we could only find out who wears shoes like this—'

'Then you'd know who shopped at Marks and Spencer,' Eddie said scornfully. 'There must be dozens of people round here who wear those. Is that the only clue you've got?'

'I—' Ashley scanned the heap of things on the table, looking for something distinctive. But there was nothing else. The letters were on ordinary paper, sent in ordinary envelopes. Written in cheap blue biro. The writing on the sheep's skull had been done in purple felt pen. And a sheep's skull might have come from anywhere. The only distinctive things were the photographs.

And how did you trace a photograph?

'There must be something else,' Sam said. 'There *has* to be.'

Eddie shrugged. 'There will be. All she's got to do is wait. He'll make a mistake in the end.'

'If he doesn't knock her off first,' Doug said heavily.

Ashley felt her throat tighten. She couldn't say a word.

'He won't try anything violent yet,' Eddie said easily. 'He hasn't worked himself up to it.' Lightly, he brushed a hand across the things on the table. 'These aren't vicious enough. Not yet.'

Sam made an odd little noise and put her hand on his arm, but he ignored her. He was looking at Ashley.

'You need one more thing,' he said softly. 'One more clue. If we follow that and then the footprints fit as well—then we'll know for sure.'

'So what do I do?' Ashley said. 'Wait? Like a human sacrifice?'

'Like a goat,' said Joe. He came out from under the table on all fours, bleating and butting at Eddie's hand with his head. But for once his imitation didn't work. Eddie pushed him away impatiently.

He was concentrating on Ashley. 'You need another clue.'

Ashley swept the things back into her carrier bag and picked it up. 'And if I get one—you'll help me?'

Eddie put out his hand. 'I promise.'

It was like a contract. 'Thank you,' Ashley said, and shook the hand.

Eddie grinned for a second and then snapped his fingers in the air. 'Who's got a car? Sam? You going to run Ashley home?'

Sam pulled a face at him, but she didn't argue. Uncoiling her long legs, she stood up. 'Come on, kid.'

'Be quick,' Eddie murmured. 'And don't let her mother see you. We don't want her asking questions. Can you go in quietly?'

Ashley nodded. 'There's a back way.'

'Fine. Don't let Sam drive like a maniac.'

Sam thumbed her nose at him and ran down the steps and across the floor. The dancers parted to let her through and Ashley followed, hearing the buzz of talking that started up behind her.

Sam didn't drive her own car as wildly as she'd driven the Hyena's, but she went much faster than

Phil. Ashley looked out anxiously for police cars, but the streets were emptier than usual.

The only person they saw was Spider Mo, trailing up Railway Street, with her hands full of bags. Sam nodded at her.

'What's Mo up to? You don't often see her out this late. She's usually bedded down somewhere by the time it's dark.,

'Maybe she got moved on,' Ashley said.

'Maybe.' Sam turned off the engine and let the car glide the last few yards down the road. 'You all right, then? Sure you can get in without waking your mother?'

'I'm fine.' Ashley picked up her bag and opened the door. 'I'll go in the back way.'

Sam nodded and lifted a hand to wave goodbye. Then she started the engine again and she was off. It sounded as though one of the parked cars had pulled away from the kerb.

Every house in the street was dark except number fourteen, where the students lived. Ashley slipped down the side of Mrs Mac's house, treading soundlessly past the shed. Opening the garden gate, she slid through like a shadow and turned to fasten the gate behind her.

As it closed, she heard a step on the other side, in the alley.

It was only one, but it was unmistakable. Someone in heavy shoes had stepped out from behind the shed. If she opened the gate again, she would see who it was.

But that would be crazy.

Instead of looking through the gate, she ran lightly across the grass, to the broken piece of fence. She was just sliding it to one side when she heard the sound of the latch. And the creak of the gate, opening again.

Her heart gave a single, huge thud, and then she was icy calm. The only sensible thing was to get inside, as quickly as possible. She squeezed through the fence with her hand in her coat pocket, feeling for the back door key. By the time she reached the door, the key was ready in her hand.

It slid into the lock—but it wouldn't turn.

Not now. Don't stick now, Ashley thought, struggling to force it round. She could hear someone feeling his way along the fence, looking for the way through.

Turn! Dropping her carrier bag, she gripped the key with both hands, leaning all her weight into the effort. It turned at last, just as the loose fence board scraped sideways. Not bothering about her bag, she wrenched the door open and fell into the kitchen, slamming the door behind her. Then she shot the bolt and sat down abruptly on the floor. Her legs were shaking too much to hold her up.

There was a long, long silence. She listened until her ears hurt, but she couldn't hear anyone coming closer. No feet crunched on the path. No hand fumbled round the lock or scraped across the door. Whoever it was, he seemed to have given up.

After ten minutes, she decided that it was ridiculous to wait any longer. Slowly and cautiously she stood up, still feeling exposed and vulnerable. The kitchen curtains hadn't been pulled right over the window, and she reached forward to tug them into place before she turned on the light.

But as she leaned across the sink, something shot upwards, suddenly, from below the window. A face—a grotesque, squashed, swollen face— jammed itself up against the glass, leering horribly at her.

There was a split second of stark, paralysed terror. Then she thought. *No! I won't! I won't be terrorized!* Grabbing up the nearest weapon she could find—the heavy rubber torch that hung by the door—she turned the key again and threw the door open.

She hadn't got anything as definite as a plan. She was just furiously, uncontrollably angry. If the face had still been there, she would have smashed the torch into it, as hard as she could.

But the man didn't wait. Even before she had the door open, he was running away, as fast as he could. She charged after him, but he made straight for the fence and crashed through it.

Common sense stopped Ashley there. Instead of following, she switched on the torch, trying to catch a glimpse of him.

All she saw was a dark anorak, but as she turned to go back inside the torch fell on a patch of colour, lying beside her abandoned carrier bag. It was a scarf. Bending down, she picked it up with the bag and took them both inside, locking the door and pulling the curtains together tightly before she put the light on.

She put the scarf down on the table, to look at it. It was a long, knitted scarf, with an odd design. Yellow and black stripes, with little black horses galloping across all the yellow stripes except the first three. They were irregular, lumpy horses, as though the person who knitted the scarf hadn't known quite how to make them look real. Certainly, there couldn't be another scarf like it in the world.

Not from Marks and Spencer, Ashley thought. And her fear dissolved into triumph. The stalker hadn't caught her. He'd given himself away and she'd got the extra piece of evidence she needed.

Now Eddie would help her!

GRANDMA

That was a joke, that scarf. His grandad knitted it for him. He was a great knitter, was Fred. Made me some lovely jumpers. One with pink roses all over it, because my name's Rose. And one with silver lurex in, for our silver wedding.

He liked jokes about names. The scarf was just to use up a load of old wool, really, but he suddenly got the idea of a joke for that as well. He'd already knitted the first few stripes, and he couldn't be bothered to unpick them, but he knitted the rest with the horses and wrapped it up as a Christmas present.

I never thought the boy would wear it, but he did. That's the funny thing about boys. When they're fourteen or fifteen, they won't touch anything that's not fashionable, but when they get a bit older there's no saying what'll take their fancy. And he loves that scarf, or he seems to. Always has it on when he comes to see me.

But then again, maybe he does it to please me. To remind me of Fred. It's the sort of thing he would do, bless him.

He's a funny boy.

18

Eddie'll fix it! Ashley thought, exultantly.

And then, from down the hall, Pauline's voice punctured her triumph.

'What's going on?'

Ashley groaned. She pushed the scarf in with the other things and hid the carrier bag behind the bread bin. Then she arranged her face into a smooth, blank mask and went along to the front room.

'Sorry, Mum. I thought I could get a drink without waking you.'

'I didn't hear you come down.'

'You were asleep,' Ashley said firmly.

That was how those conversations always went. As long as she didn't waver, Pauline would believe her. Or pretend she did, anyway.

There was a silence. Then Pauline said, 'Was I snoring, then?'

'Like a lion,' Ashley said cheerfully. 'I thought it would be quite safe if I slipped down and—'

'No you didn't!'

'What?' Ashley was so startled that she nearly let her mouth drop open. But she managed to keep up the mask. 'Sorry?' she said again. Politely puzzled, this time.

'You're lying,' Pauline said. 'Put the light on. I want to see your face.'

'But you need to sleep—'

'No I don't. I need to talk.'

Reluctantly, Ashley flicked the light switch. She saw her mother look her up and down, taking in what she was wearing.

'I was just getting a drink,' she said quickly, before Pauline could comment. And she gave her the blank, open-eyed stare that usually fixed things.

'So why are you dressed?' Pauline said. 'And what were you doing out in the garden?'

There was a longer silence. This time, Ashley took in her mother's fierce, determined expression. Something had changed. She wasn't sure she could stare her down any more.

Pauline patted the bed beside her. 'Come and sit here.'

'I really ought to go back to sleep—'

'If you don't come here now,' Pauline said evenly, 'I'll phone Janet up. This minute. At two o'clock in the morning. I'll say I can't cope any more and you'll have to go and live with her.'

'You wouldn't!'

'Oh yes, I would. It's only the truth. You're always

going out at night and pretending that you haven't. You could be getting into all sorts of trouble. Meeting boys, and taking drugs, and—'

'Oh, for goodness' sake!' Ashley's calm finally broke. 'Do you think I'm that stupid? I wouldn't—'

'How do I know?'

They had both spoken more loudly than they meant to, and Mrs Macdonald hammered on her bedroom floor. But they hardly heard her. They were facing each other like enemies.

And all the time, Ashley was thinking frantically, *I can't tell her! I can't, I can't, I can't!*

'Well?' Pauline said.

Ashley never remembered hearing her voice sound so strong. So confident. But that only made it worse. If she knew everything, that might all collapse into ruins. They'd be back where they were before.

Ashley sat down on the bed. 'I wasn't going to tell you,' she said slowly.

'No kidding?' Pauline's voice was bitter and sarcastic. 'Do you ever tell me anything?'

'I'm only trying not to upset you!' Suddenly, Ashley saw a way of managing. A way of telling the truth— or some of it—without risking too much. She leaned forward. 'I suppose you ought to know, though. The last few evenings there's been . . . well, there's been someone in the garden. At night.'

171

'What sort of someone?' Pauline said cautiously.

'I don't know who he is, but—' Ashley jumped up. Now she'd worked out what to do, it was hard to keep herself from gabbling. 'Wait a minute, and I'll show you.'

She ran into the kitchen and pulled out the scarf, and the drawing of the footprint. Then she ran back and dropped them on to the bed.

'Look. These are the footprints he left. Joe drew the pattern so we could show Eddie Beale. That's where I went tonight. To see Eddie and ask if he would help. When I came back someone was lurking in the alley, and he dropped this scarf.'

She was talking deliberately fast, to shut out any questions. Pauline picked up the scarf, looking bewildered.

'Who's Eddie Beale? And what's he got to do with all this?'

'He's . . . ' Ashley faltered for a moment. 'He's a friend of Tricia's. And he knows everyone. He knows everything that's going on.'

'But why ask him? Why not phone the police?'

'The police?' Ashley made herself sound incredulous. 'What's the point? They never found out who burgled the chip shop last year, did they? They couldn't even catch the people who put Tony Cavalieri into a wheelchair. They're useless.'

Pauline ran the scarf through her hands. 'And you think this Eddie Beale can do better?'

'That's what Joe says. And Vikki does too. They say Eddie knows everyone, and he can always find out what's going on.'

Pauline frowned. 'And this scarfs going to help?' She turned it over, examining the other side. 'It looks rather familiar.'

'You've seen it?' Ashley was startled.

'I think so. Or maybe I've heard someone talking about it. There's some kind of story . . . ' Pauline frowned harder, trying to remember. 'It's no use. It's gone. Maybe Eddie can find out. But I still wish you'd phone the police.'

'Let's try this first. Please.' Ashley caught at her mother's arm. 'If Eddie finds out who it is, he'll just warn him off. And I won't have to go to court or anything. It'll save such a lot of fuss.'

Pauline wavered for a moment, and then she nodded. 'I suppose it won't do any harm. As long as there's no more trouble. But you'd better make sure the back door's locked and bolted.'

Ashley hadn't worked out how to contact Eddie. On the way back from school that afternoon, she watched out for Joe, but there was no sign of him. As she came along the Row, she was wondering whether her mother knew Tricia's telephone number.

Then she turned the corner into Railway Street and she knew she didn't have to bother about any of that. Eddie was at her house, waiting for her. She could tell, from the far end of the street.

It wasn't just the big car double-parked outside. It wasn't even the noise of the radio, coming from the front room. She guessed that he was there when she saw the children hanging around in little groups.

They were pretending to kick a ball about, or do a bit of skate-boarding, but it was all half-hearted. Really, they wanted to know what was going on, and why Eddie Beale had come to visit. As she pushed her way through, to get to the front door, she could hear them whispering his name.

The door wasn't even closed properly. She pushed it open and marched into the house. Even above the noise of the radio, she could hear Tricia and her mother giggling. And there was another woman's voice as well.

It was Sam. She was draped over the end of the bed, gulping with laughter as she pretended to pose. Joe was leaping around in front of her, with an imaginary camera, pulling intense, ridiculous faces.

'That's *fabulous*, sweetheart. *Really* sexy. But we need a bigger pout. And some more glare. Give it all your *glare*, Sammy. And the chin. The chin needs to be a *teensy* bit higher—'

They didn't even realize that Ashley had come in, but Eddie saw her. He was sitting at the table, watching everything with a detached, ironic stare. As Ashley came through the door, he moved one hand sharply, signalling to the others. *Stop.*

Joe broke off in mid-word and Tricia and Sam stopped laughing instantly. Only Pauline looked puzzled for a second. Then she saw Ashley in the doorway and she smiled.

'Hallo, Ash,' she said. 'Guess what? Tricia dropped in for a cup of tea, so I told her you wanted to see Eddie. And she phoned him straight away.'

'Hi.' Ashley raised a hand, feeling suddenly shy of Eddie now that he was in her house.

If he noticed, he ignored it. He didn't even waste time saying hallo. He picked up the black and yellow scarf from the table in front of him and ran it through his hands.

'Your mother says you've had someone round the back of the house again,' he said carefully. His eyes were bright and sharp, and Ashley understood what he meant. *We haven't told your mother the rest.*

Ashley nodded, cautiously. 'He chased me in last night. And he dropped that scarf when he ran away.'

'Did you see his face?' Eddie said sharply.

'I . . . sort of. He jammed it against the kitchen window, but it was all swollen and squashed up.'

'Stocking over his head,' said Sam. 'Probably an improvement on his real face.'

Eddie turned the scarf over in his hands. 'You're probably right. If this scarf belongs to the person I think it does.'

Ashley's fists clenched, and Pauline leaned forward.

'You know who it is?'

'Maybe.'

'Who?' Ashley said. '*Tell* me!'

Eddie shook his head. 'Not yet. I want to be sure. I want *you* to be sure. I think we'll do a little test. Here!' He screwed the scarf into a ball and tossed it across the room to Joe. 'Put that on.'

Joe draped the scarf round his neck, tucking it inside his jacket. Eddie made an impatient movement.

'Not like that. Spread it out. So people can see the pattern.'

When it was rearranged, Joe had black horses galloping lumpily all the way across his chest. Eddie gave an approving nod.

'Go on then. Up to the Row and into all the shops. See what reaction you get. And take Ashley with you.'

They went, obediently. Ashley had forgotten the children round the door and she almost fell over one of the little ones. Dean Fox, from across the road. But he didn't fuss. He was much too interested in what was going on.

DEAN

'Course we wanted to know what was up. I mean— you don't expect to see Eddie Beale hanging round here in the daytime, do you? And you certainly don't expect to see him in Super-Ashley's house. Super oh-how-all-the-old-ladies-love-her Ashley. When Steve said Eddie was there, I thought he was conning me. But I hung around to see, anyway, in case he was right. When Eddie's around, something always happens.

The first thing that happened was Ashley coming home from school. She went straight in the house, but she didn't stay long. A couple of minutes later she was out again, with that kid who hangs round with Eddie. The kid whose mother lives with Vince Rowlands. He was wearing a huge great striped scarf.

'Hey, Waspy!' I said, without thinking. 'Off to sting someone?'

Steve nudged me, to tell me not to be so thick. Whatever the kid was doing, it was probably something for Eddie, and Eddie doesn't like people snooping. But it was OK. The kid looked round and pointed a finger to zap me, but he didn't look annoyed. He just went on up the road, with Ashley.

And we all followed him, of course.

They walked up to the Row and started mooching in and out of the shops. It was weird. They didn't buy anything, but they weren't pinching things either. (That would have been a laugh. Super-Ashley on the lift. I wish.) And they didn't seem to mind being followed.

Just as well, really. The further they went, the more kids they collected. There must have been fifteen or twenty of us by the time they walked into Fat Annie's.

And that was where it happened. Straight away, the minute they walked in. Annie looked up from the till and saw the scarf the kid was wearing and she went berserk. Turned bright purple and bellowed across the shop.

'Hey! You! What are you doing with my son's scarf?'

19

Ashley was three or four steps behind Joe, and Annie obviously thought she was just one of the crowd. Ignoring Ashley, she concentrated all her fury on Joe. She came marching across the shop and wrenched the scarf off his neck, tugging so hard she nearly choked him.

'Thieving little—can't leave things around for a moment without someone grabbing them. Greed, that's what's wrong with the world today. Greed and no morals. Now get out of my shop. And don't come back!'

Tossing the scarf down behind the counter, she seized Joe's collar and began to haul him towards the door, through the crowds of people who had edged in behind him.

Ashley would have followed but, as Joe went past, he turned his head towards her, away from Annie. He was mouthing a single word.

Shoes.

For a moment, Ashley couldn't work out what he meant. Then, when he reached the door, he lifted his foot and shook it at her, exposing the sole. He was telling her to check out the footprints.

For the first time, Ashley took in what they had discovered. It was the Hyena's scarf.

But it can't be. It can't be the Hyena who did all those things.

It was his scarf.

She stood quite still and watched Annie struggling to get Joe over the threshold. All the kids outside were jostling her and jeering.

'What's the matter, Mrs Galt?'

'Did he steal the scarf, then?'

'Lovely scarf, innit? Wish I had one with dear little gee- gees all over it.'

'Want me to bash him for you, missus?'

Dear little gee-gees, Ashley thought. *G.G.s*

She felt someone staring at her. Turning to look back into the shop, she saw the Hyena coming out of the stockroom. Before she could react, he was smiling at her.

She stepped sideways, trying to get out of his line of sight, and her elbow caught a shelf full of chocolate bars. She knocked the first one out of place and the rest of them began to rain down on the floor, in an avalanche of red and brown wrappings.

'Oh, I'm sorry!' She bent down and started to scoop them up, frantically.

'It's all right. Please don't— Let me—' The Hyena knelt down beside her and grabbed at the bars, to stop her picking them up. She jumped away from him and stood up.

And there were the soles that had made the footprints in her garden.

There was no mistake. She knew the pattern by heart now. Three curves to each wave. Four waves on the sole and two on the heel. Six dots in between the front waves, and four nearer the back. Size ten or eleven at least.

It didn't seem real. But when she looked again, the pattern was still there. There was no doubt about it. The Hyena's shoes had left the footprints. The Hyena's scarf had been dropped in her garden.

He must be the stalker. The man who had sneaked into her garden and bashed at the sheep's skull until it splintered and broke. The one who had crouched under her bedroom window, by the drainpipe. The one who took those photos, and then drew on them . . .

The person who knew who she was.

She had to get out of the shop. Fast. Dropping the chocolate bars she was holding, she started for the door.

He bleated after her. 'Wait a moment! Wasn't there . . . um . . . wasn't there something—?'

'Nothing, thanks.' She shouted it without turning

round. The idea of looking at him was unbearable. 'I've changed my mind.'

There were even more people hanging around outside now. Kids from the flats, who'd come down when they saw the crowd. Ashley pushed her way through them and ran down the road to where Joe was standing.

'You were great!' he called, before she reached him. 'That was a brilliant idea with the Mars Bars. Did he have the right shoes?'

Ashley didn't want to answer with all the kids standing round. But her head was whirling, and she had to speak. To share it with someone. 'He . . . he . . . I saw—'

She could tell, from the way people were staring at her, that she looked peculiar, and she tried to calm down. But Joe wouldn't leave her alone.

'It was him,' he said. 'Wasn't it?'

There were strange kids everywhere, pressing in on her. Crowding nearer, with their mouths open and their ears flapping, trying to hear what her answer would be. She had just enough sense left to realize that she mustn't say any more. Pushing past Joe, she began to hurry home. Not quite running, but marching fast, with her hands in her pockets and her head down. She must get home. That was all she could think. She had to get home and see Eddie.

But Eddie hadn't hung around there. She was only halfway down the road when his car came gliding up towards her. Sam waved and pulled into the kerb. Eddie was in the back, with a can of beer, and he leaned across and pushed the door open.

'Get in,' he said.

Ashley hesitated and Joe pushed at her shoulder. 'Go on!' he said. 'It's better than talking with your mother there.'

They slid in and Eddie flicked at Joe's shoulders, where the scarf had been.

'Well?'

'We found the owner,' Joe said. 'He—'

'It *can't* be him!' Ashley said fiercely. 'It's nonsense.'

Eddie raised his eyebrows. 'No? What about the shoes? Did you check those?'

'Yes I did, but—'

'So what's your problem?'

She didn't know. She looked down at her fingers, plaiting them together in her lap.

There was a straggle of kids coming down the road now, looking curiously at Eddie's car. He leaned forward and tapped Sam on the shoulder.

'Drive round the block a couple of times. Then we'll take Ashley home.'

Sam nodded, put the car into gear and drove off. As they reached the Row, Ashley turned her head away, to avoid seeing Fat Annie's. She met Eddie's eyes.

'I'll tell you why you won't believe it,' he said silkily. 'It's because you know him, isn't it? You can't cope with it being someone you know.'

That was part of it. But there was more than that. 'It's not just because I know him. It's . . . how can *he* be the one who knows me? Like that? It's unbelievable. If I hadn't seen—'

'But you did see.' Eddie's voice was still silky, but it was relentless. 'He's the one who's been stalking you all right.'

'But . . . what am I going to do? Even if he stops, I'll see him every day. I'll know he said those things.'

'He hasn't got to be there,' Eddie said softly.

For a moment, Ashley didn't know what he meant. Her mouth fell open, and she imagined nightmares.

Death.

'Don't be silly,' Eddie said impatiently, so that she knew he had read her mind. 'There's no need for anything heavy. You've got him over a barrel. He's a shopkeeper.'

'So?' Ashley hadn't got a clue what he was talking about.

'Spell it out for her, Joe.'

Joe tossed his head, shaking imaginary curls. 'You've only got to tell people, you know.' His voice rose an octave. 'I'm not going *there* again! Not if he's been stalking that poor little girl. I mean—you could get *murdered*, couldn't you? And I'm certainly not sending my children! We'll do our shopping somewhere else from now on!'

'You see?' Eddie said softly. 'That's all it takes. The shop will go bust, and he and Annie will have to sell it and move.'

'But that's—' Ashley swallowed. 'That's not fair. Why should Annie suffer?'

There was a sniff from the front of the car. '*Poor* Annie.' Sam's voice was like vinegar. 'And she's so gentle and kind, too.'

'Yeah,' Joe said. 'Leave her alone, Ash. What does it matter if the Hyena bashes your head in? You can't be mean to Annie, can you?'

Eddie didn't say anything. He just waited.

Ashley plaited her fingers harder. 'But . . . he wouldn't really *hurt* me.'

'No?' Eddie shrugged. 'Well, you can believe that if you like. But stalkers do hurt people. Quite often.'

Ashley tried to imagine the Hyena hurting her. Putting his hands round her neck. Sticking a knife between her ribs. Her brain wouldn't make the pictures.

'So what are you going to do?' Eddie said. He dropped his beer can on to the floor and crunched it suddenly under his foot. The metal twisted into sharp, ugly creases. 'All you have to do is say yes, and I'll do the rest. I can put the word about, as long as you don't deny it. Do you want that?'

Ashley looked at the beer can. In her head, she saw the Hyena's heavy foot coming down like that, on top of the sheep's skull. She saw the bone splinter. And she thought, *That could be my skull.*

'Yes,' she said. It took an effort, but she didn't see what else she could say. 'Yes. Tell everyone.'

There was no time to think again. Eddie nodded briskly and Sam whipped round the final corner and pulled up outside Ashley's house.

'Tell Tricia and Doug we're going,' Eddie said.

Ashley nodded and dived out of the car. There were kids outside her house again, but she ignored them all, even the ones she knew. She wanted to be inside, away from everyone.

NADINE

She just dived into the house, without saying a word. And that made it even more mysterious. I couldn't work out what was going on.

I thought it was a fight at first, when I saw the crowd outside Fat Annie's. I was up in Diane's flat, minding her kids, and Kimberley called out from the window.

186

'Look! Look!'

Then she made for the door. She's only six, and there's nothing she likes better than watching a punch-up.

She was out of the flat and into the lift before I could stop her. I picked up Carl and chased after her, but I didn't catch up until we reached the cinema. And even then I couldn't persuade her to go back. She dragged me over the road to Fat Annie's.

Annie was throwing a boy out of the shop. Everyone was yelling and screaming and Kimberley started laughing like a maniac. The minute Annie went back inside, the boy darted over to the shop window and peered in.

That's when I noticed the girl.

It was that girl from Railway Street. She was in the shop, and she was bending over, picking something up. Mr Galt was there too, helping her, and when the boy saw that, he grinned—you've never seen such a huge grin—and punched the air, like, YESS!

A second later, the girl came running out, and he was on to her in a flash.

'Great idea with the Mars Bars! What about his shoes?'

Shoes? There must have been twenty or thirty kids there, and we all stopped yelling, because we wanted to know what shoes had got to do with anything. But the girl didn't say a word. She charged off towards her house and the boy ran after her.

And so did Kimberley.

That child's a menace. The minute I let go of her hand, she was away. I dodged after her, with Carl kicking my ribs to bits, but I didn't catch her until halfway down Railway Street. And there was the girl, getting into a car.

Eddie Beale's car.

If Eddie Beale's involved, there must be a story somewhere. But we didn't find out what it was, even though we all went and waited outside the girl's house. Like I said, she swept in like a film star. With no comment written all over her face. I felt like kicking the front door down.

You know how it is with a story. You've got to hear the end. She can no comment all she likes, but I'm going to find out what's going on. I'll go mad if I don't.

There were loads of kids outside the shop. They saw everything, and they feel just the same as me. Someone's going to get the story, sooner or later ...

20

Tell everyone, Ashley had said. But she'd never thought it could happen so fast. The next morning, when she was on her way to school, Lisa came bouncing up to her.

'Is that right? The Hyena's been stalking you?'

Ashley was caught off balance, and she just muttered something. But when the second person asked—and the third, and the fourth—she gathered her wits.

'I don't want any trouble,' she whispered. 'I can't say—'

That was all it took. No lies. Not even any need to tell the truth. Dozens of people had seen the business with the scarf and they were all desperate to know what was going on. By lunchtime, pretty well everyone in the school knew that Ashley was being stalked by the man from Fat Annie's. And that she wouldn't talk about it.

'They think you're scared silly,' Vikki said.

All through break, she hovered round, protecting Ashley, and at lunchtime she called in reinforcements. Matt. From the moment they left class, he was just behind Ashley, ready to sort out anyone who tried to speak to her.

If it hadn't been so irritating, it would have been funny. Matt was six foot two and very tough, but Vikki was determined to make him run round after Ashley. She stood there and stamped her foot, until he agreed.

'You're not to let people annoy her!' she said fiercely. 'She's got enough to put up with, without people going on at her. If anyone wants to know about the stalking, *I'll* tell them.'

And that was how it was. When the bell went, Matt ushered Ashley into lunch and stood beside her, like a sentry. If people tried to talk, he glared at them and once or twice he even took a threatening step forward. That was as far as it went, though. No one wanted to tangle with Matt.

Meanwhile, Vikki was having the time of her life, spreading the story to everyone who hadn't got the details. 'Yes!' Ashley heard her saying. Over and over again. 'There was a smashed skull. And photographs with *horrible* things scrawled on them. And he peered in at the kitchen window!'

Everyone was getting the message. And Vikki made sure they remembered it when they went home.

'Matt'll walk you back,' she said to Ashley. 'Won't you, Matt?'

'It's OK,' Ashley said faintly. 'Really. I don't need—'

'Of course you do!' Vikki was determined. 'Suppose you met the Hyena? You've got to be careful, Ash.'

After school, she and Matt both marched Ashley through the estate and past the cinema.

'Keep on the outside,' Vikki said. 'While we're going past the shop. You don't want him staring at you.'

But by the time they reached the traffic lights, they could see there wasn't a problem. The pavement outside Fat Annie's was crowded.

'What are they doing?' Ashley said.

Vikki pulled a face. 'They're ghouls, aren't they? Come to take a look at the Monster.'

'You mean—all those people know about the stalking?'

'Of course they do,' Matt said. 'Come on, Ashley. *Everyone* knows.'

'That's why there's no one *inside* the shop!' Vikki said triumphantly.

She was peering through the window as they passed. The Hyena was at the till and as she spoke he glanced up at the crowd outside, obviously puzzled. He caught Vikki's eye and she pulled a face and looked away.

'Yuck! Did you see him?' She put an arm round Ashley's shoulders, hustling her away. 'I'd like to go in there and tell him just what I think!'

She half-turned, as if she meant it, and Matt looked anguished.

'Victoria! You mustn't! If he starts noticing you—'

The sentence broke off, as if it was too frightening to finish. Matt began to hurry both of them, slipping slightly behind, as if he wanted to block the Hyena's view.

'It's OK,' Ashley said feebly. 'I'm sure he won't do anything.'

Matt took no notice. Once he made up his mind he was impossible to shift. 'It'll be better if you don't walk home this way,' he said. 'It's not much further if you go round the top of the estate. And Ashley can go into the Spar up there. Can't you, Ash?'

'I . . . suppose so.' It was the first time Ashley had thought about shopping. The Spar was another ten minutes walk away, but it was the only choice she had.

Vikki was already organizing her.

'If you bring your list into school, we can come with you. And Matt can carry the shopping.'

Matt nodded vigorously. 'We can go home together every day, if you like.'

'I really don't think you need to.'

'Of course we do!' Vikki's arm tightened. 'We're your friends, aren't we?'

She wasn't taking any chances. She and Matt

marched stoutly down the road, all the way to Ashley's front door. One on each side.

'We'll leave you when you're safe,' Vikki said. 'When we've checked there's nothing . . . *unusual* going on.'

But when they reached the house, a cheerful voice called out as Ashley opened the front door.

'Come *in*, sweetheart! Pauline and I are playing Scrabble, and I'm *destroying* her!'

'What the—' Matt's eyes opened very wide. Then he stuck his head round the front room door and laughed. 'Oh, it's you. Hi, Joe.'

As they went into the room, Pauline looked up and grinned. 'Hallo, Vikki. Hallo, Matt. You know Joe, do you? He's a terrible cheat!'

Vikki just laughed, but Matt obviously knew Joe properly, because he went to read the words on the board. '*Inax? Klooga? Mzaarg*? What's the matter, pie-face? Can't you read?'

'You just don't understand the creative mind!' Joe threw himself back in the chair, spreading his arms flamboyantly. 'I like to expand the language!'

'I think my mind's expanded enough.' Pauline pushed her letter rack aside. 'My waist wants a turn now. Nip up to the shop and get some crumpets will you, Ashie?'

There was an instant of utter stillness.

Then Vikki reacted. 'Matt can go.'

'No, it's OK—' Ashley said.

But Vikki had already taken the money Pauline was holding out, and she was packing Matt off through the front door.

'If you run, you can go to the Spar instead, and she'll never know. You'll be back before we've made the tea.'

She slammed the door behind him and then followed Ashley down the hall, into the kitchen. But she wasn't really interested in helping with the tea. She opened the back door.

'Shall I take a look in the garden? In case there's . . . you know. In case he's been there.'

'You don't need to,' Ashley said quickly.

But it was too late already. They had both seen the envelope, just outside the back door.

'Don't touch it,' Ashley muttered.

But Vikki couldn't resist it. She bent down and picked up the envelope. 'Hey, it's *heavy*.'

'Don't—' Ashley said again, uselessly.

Vikki ignored her and ripped the flap open. Ashley saw a quick flash of red, and then Vikki sucked in a huge, terrified breath and opened her mouth to scream.

Ashley got there just in time. She jammed her hand over Vikki's mouth and hissed in her ear. 'Be quiet! Be *quiet*! Or my mum will hear.'

Shuddering, Vikki pushed the envelope at her, wriggling free and backing away. There was a polythene bag in it, with a red mess sealed inside. As Ashley took it, the polythene bag tipped out on to the table, falling flat so that they could see the crimson shape inside. Perfectly sculpted. Oozing blood round the edges.

It was cut into a neat heart shape, like something from a Valentine card, but without the prettiness. Raw and ugly. Vikki was staring at it with her eyes wide.

'What is it?' she whispered.

Ashley forced herself to look. Forced herself to stretch out and prod at the polythene. The package squashed under her finger in a soft, familiar way.

'It's OK,' she said. 'It's only raw liver. Look.'

'Only!' Vikki pulled a face. 'It's disgusting.'

Ashley picked up the polythene bag by one edge.

'Yuck!' Vikki whispered. 'Oh *yuck!* Get rid of it!'

It went straight into the dustbin outside. And Ashley made them both strong cups of tea, laced with sugar.

MATT
Victoria hasn't got a clue how serious all this is. It's a game to her. She likes a bit of drama, but she doesn't know how tough things are, out in the streets. She's just playing at looking after Ash.

I wish she hadn't got mixed up in it.

Who's to say he'll stick to stalking Ashley? I mean, Ash is OK, but next to Victoria—there's no comparison, is there? If he starts turning his snoopy eyes on Vikki, I'll . . . I'll—

I went past Annie's on my way to the Spar. The crowds had gone and it looked pretty empty in there. He was standing at the counter, looking as if he didn't know what to do with himself.

I really wanted to go in there and punch him. I wanted to get him by the throat and say: What d'you mean by it? Why don't you knock it off?

The Spar was full of people when I got there, and I had to queue to pay, but I didn't care about that. I'm not going into Annie's again.

And I'll tell my mates to lay off it too. Maybe Ginger can spread the word about a bit. She knows lots of people, especially now she's going out with Phil. And she's always asking me about Ashley, too. She ought to take an interest in what's happening to her.

It shows us up, having something like that happening round here. If we don't get rid of him, it'll look as if anyone can push us around.

We've got to get him out.

21

'You can't stay in this house,' Vikki said. 'You can't!' She curled her hands round the cup of tea and Ashley could see the surface of the liquid shivering.

'So what do we do?' she said. 'Book a room at the Ritz? We haven't got anywhere else to go, Vik.'

'But it's not safe!'

'Keep your voice down.' Ashley poured her own tea, and some for Pauline and Joe. 'It was only a bit of liver, you know. Just a cheap trick.'

'It was *horrible!*' Vikki shuddered.

'I told you not to touch it.' Ashley sat down at the table beside her. 'Look, I'm sorry you had a shock, but it's nearly over. Now we know who it is, he's not going to be around for long. If Eddie's right.'

'Of course he's right!' Vikki said. 'You wait till I start telling people about the liver. No one's going to go near that shop!'

'You can't tell every single person.'

'I don't need to. People are all telling each other. It's spreading like a forest fire.'

There was a loud knock on the door. Vikki jumped up, eager with relief.

'That's Matt! I'll go and let him in!'

Ashley sat and thought about forest fires. And the way they spread.

Vikki hadn't been exaggerating. By Saturday morning, the story had reached Janet.

Ashley knew she'd heard, the moment she saw her. She arrived with the twins, as they'd arranged, at half-past ten and when Ashley opened the door, Karen and Louise were on the doorstep, bouncing up and down as usual. Janet was beside them, with a bunch of flowers in her hand as if she'd come to visit someone in hospital. And behind her was Frank, who almost never came.

Janet erupted over the doorstep.

'Oh, *Ashley!* Why didn't you—?'

Frank prodded her arm—*not in front of the twins*—and she stopped elaborately, clapping a hand over her mouth. Then she put on her brightest smile.

'In you go then, girls! I bet Mummy's dying to show you her new hairstyle!'

That worked straight away for Karen. She gave a loud whoop and threw herself over the doorstep and across the hall. Louise didn't move so fast. She looked up at Ashley.

'It's OK,' Ashley said. 'Come in, Lou. Mum's been waiting for you.'

She would have liked to keep Louise there, as a shield against Frank and Janet, but that wasn't fair. And anyway, if Janet wanted to talk to her she would make sure she did, sooner or later. Better to get it over.

But Janet wasn't going to start until she'd been through the whole greetings ceremony. She swooped into the front room, stopped dead and let out a delighted shriek.

'Paulie, you look fabulous! Absolutely elegant, and so *well!* You should have had your hair cut years ago!'

Pauline reached for her sticks, but Janet wouldn't let her stand up.

'Don't move. The girls will tell you what they've been up to. Frank and I are going to take a look at the garden. With Ashley. She can tell us *all your news.'*

It was obvious what she meant. And just in case Pauline had missed the point, she finished with a long, sympathetic stare. Ashley was terrified that she was going to go on, but the twins interrupted her, bouncing across the room.

'You look great, Mummy!' Karen said. 'You look brilliant! Let's have our hair cut like that, Lou!'

Louise didn't answer. She was staring, and stretching out one finger to touch the short curls at the back of her mother's neck.

'Don't you like it?' Pauline said.

Louise looked at her, without smiling. 'What did they do with your hair? After they cut it off?'

'I kept it for you!' Pauline said. 'One for you, and one for Karen. Look!'

She pulled open the drawer beside the table and lifted out two long plaits. Ashley had a pang of such jealousy that she could hardly speak. *That's mine*! she wanted to say. She'd brushed that hair and teased out the tangles and plaited it, for years and years and years. But her mother wasn't going to give *her* a plait. She hadn't even told her they were there.

'Oh, how sweet!' Janet was cooing.

Louise reached for a plait and a huge smile spread across her face, showing the gap between her front teeth. And Ashley thought, *I wasn't much older than that when Mum started being ill.*

Turning away abruptly, she headed into the kitchen, to give Janet an excuse to follow and talk to her. Janet seized the opportunity.

'Let's go and look at the garden now, Frank. Ashley can show us if there's anything that needs doing.'

She swept them both in front of her, down the hall. As Frank stepped into the kitchen, Ashley saw him wince at the broken shelves and the worn-out floor. He hated shabbiness. Hurriedly he pushed the back door open and went out into the garden.

It was obvious, immediately, that there was nothing

200

that needed doing. The grass had stopped growing for the winter, and Ashley had pruned the roses a month ago. But they all knew that the garden was only an excuse. They were going to have A Talk.

Janet closed the back door with dramatic care. Then she turned and flung her arms round Ashley, knocking the breath out of her.

'Oh, you poor little *thing!* Why didn't you ring us? Why didn't you *say*? You must have been having a dreadful time.'

Over her shoulder, Ashley could see Frank's face puckering, as though he felt slightly sick.

'I . . . it's all *right*,' she gasped. 'I'm fine, honestly.'

'But you must have been so terrified!' Janet loosened her grip and stood back, looking earnestly into Ashley's eyes. 'Ever since Mrs Macdonald rang me up last night, I haven't been able to rest, thinking of it. I didn't close my eyes for a moment last night, did I, Frank?'

Frank shook his head stiffly and turned away to walk round the garden. Looking for evidence, Ashley thought. Janet glanced at him and then leaned closer, whispering.

'Don't you take any notice of that. He's just as upset as I am, but—you know how men are. He's very keen to help, though.'

'There's nothing to *do*,' Ashley said. 'Honestly. It's just a silly thing—'

'Have you been to the police?'

'I—' Ashley thought fast. She didn't want Janet latching on to that. 'I *can't* go to the police. I don't want to worry Mum.'

Janet stared. 'What do you mean? You haven't told her?'

'Only a bit. She knows someone's been lurking round the back of the house, but that's all. It's not good for her to worry.' That was true, but it was a cheap excuse. Ashley looked down at her feet, hating herself for it.

It worked, though. Janet patted her arm with a hand that trembled slightly. 'You're a good, brave girl. But you must be careful.'

'I am.' Ashley went on looking at her feet. 'There hasn't been anything dangerous, really. He just followed me home one night—'

'That's your own fault,' Frank said sourly, coming back down the garden. 'It's asking for trouble, going out after dark.'

It's dark when I walk home from school, Ashley wanted to say. But it would be silly to annoy him. She smiled meekly.

'No, Uncle Frank.'

'And you ought to keep away from that man. And the shop. Get your groceries somewhere else.'

'Yes, Uncle Frank.'

'And you must *talk to us*,' Janet squeezed Ashley's arm. 'Learning something like that from an outsider was—well, it was hurtful. You *must* phone up and keep us in touch, Ashie. And if things get worse, *we'll* go to the police.'

Ashley nodded, but she didn't mean it. There was no way of explaining things to Janet. She hadn't got a clue what it was like, living by the Row.

'It sounds as if Ashley's going to be quite safe. As long as she's sensible.' Frank's voice was clipped and chilly. 'No point in making unnecessary fuss. Now how about some coffee? I don't want to hang about too long.'

They only stayed an hour. And when they went, there was a long brown plait, left lying on the couch.

'That's Karen's,' Ashley said. 'Do you want me to—?'

'Oh, leave it!' Pauline said, irritably. 'It can go in the bin if she doesn't want it.'

She was tired and petulant. When she wasn't looking, Ashley coiled up the plait and pushed it into her pocket. Then she fetched a dustpan and started to brush the crumbs off the carpet, before she forgot and trod them in.

'Leave that, Ash. I want to talk to you.'

'It won't take a minute—'

'LEAVE IT!'

Ashley dropped the dustpan and sat back on her heels. 'What's the matter?'

Pauline put a hand into her cardigan pocket. 'This came through the door. Karen picked it up while you were in the garden with Frank and Janet.'

Even before she pulled out the envelope, Ashley knew what it would look like. Long and brown. *But not liver*, she thought frantically. *Please not liver*.

It wasn't liver. Just another piece of paper. Pauline pulled it out.

'I thought it was a circular or something,' she said. 'That's why I opened it.'

Ashley held out a hand, but her mother didn't pass the paper over. She spread it out and held it up for Ashley to see. The message had been cut out of newspaper and stuck on, in whole words and single letters.

CinDY

You've gOt such tHin BONEs. You'VE got suCH Red BLOOD. YOU CAN't cARry On Like thaT. YouLL Fall.

FRANK
I reckon Ashley's made the whole thing up.
I've always had a feeling about that girl. She's too

good to be true. Whatever you say, she smiles and agrees with you, but you can't tell what's going on in that head of hers. Give me our Karrie, any day, I say. She may be a bit of a madam, but you know where you are with her. Even Lulu will climb up on your knee and tell you what's the matter with her. But Ashley—she's devious. And she's itching for attention. You can see it in her face.

Janet won't hear a word against her, of course. She's always going on at me to talk to Pauline and tell her it's not fair to make Ashley work so hard. Janet reckons she ought to come and live with us. But I'm not having any of that.

'You don't know when you're well off,' I say. 'We've got our girls—isn't that enough for you?'

Because Karrie and Lulu are our girls really. We've had them since they were born, or very nearly. I don't know why Janet keeps up this nonsense of taking them to see Pauline. They haven't got the link with her. Not any more.

And it doesn't do them any good to drag them to a place like that. The house is bad enough, and the neighbourhood's worse. All that filth and graffiti. And the way people stare. We stopped off at the shops, and there was a man staring down at us from one of the windows upstairs. I don't want Karen and Louise dragged into all that, and there's no need. We've got the twins, and Pauline's got Ashley, and it all works fine.

It's true Pauline's hard up, but she can't really expect us to do any more. And we're certainly not taking on Little Miss Ashley Ice Cream.

She's the sort that puts on a good performance, but you never know what's going on inside her head. If you really want to know, I'm sorry for that chap in the shop. He's probably smiled at her a couple of times, and she's built up the whole thing in her imagination. He's in for trouble, if you ask me.

And the shop's suffering already. We stopped off there because Janet wanted to take a look at the man, so I said why not buy some flowers for Pauline. But there was no man there. Just a fat woman. And the flowers were rubbish. Jan had a job finding a bunch that wasn't wilting. The fruit and vegetables were past their best as well.

If you ask me, that shop's in a bad way.

22

CinDY

You've gOt such tHin BONEs. You'VE got suCH
Red BLOOD. YOU CAN't cARry on Like thaT.
YouLL Fall.

For a split second—just the faintest flicker of time—
Ashley looked at the pasted newspaper letters and
thought she was going to tell her mother the whole
thing.

Then common sense took over.

'It must be a mistake,' she said quickly. 'Look, it's
not for me at all. It says Cindy.'

Pauline gave her a long look. 'Who's that?'

'Cindy? She's—' Ashley knew it was boasting, but
she couldn't resist the temptation. 'She's a climber.
No one knows who she is, but she gets into the most
extraordinary places—really high—and writes her
name there, to show she's been.'

Pauline frowned. 'You mean—graffiti?'

'Sort of. Only with lots of colours and shading and
stuff.'

Ashley felt her face going pink. Quickly she turned
away and picked up the dustpan again.

'Shall I get the lunch?'

She could feel Pauline's brain working. Adding things up. Maybe it was best to be out of the way. Scooping the last few crumbs into the pan, she headed for the door, but she didn't quite make it in time.

'Ashley?'

'Mmm?' Ashley didn't look round.

'What's going on?'

It wasn't an ordinary question. Ashley knew Pauline was watching her and she answered smoothly, without turning round.

'Some kid's obviously decided I'm Cindy. Maybe they've seen me climbing in gym. I'm pretty good at it. Or maybe it's not only me who's got a letter like that. Perhaps someone's delivered lots, to all sorts of people. To see who reacts. Shall I ask Vikki if she's got one too?'

Pauline hesitated. Then she folded the letter up and slipped it back into the envelope. 'That might be a good idea. Take it and show her. Here.'

She held the letter out, and Ashley was forced to turn round, to take it. But by then she had her face under control.

Until Pauline said, 'Ashie—'

It wasn't the word. It was the way she said it, as if she were talking to someone really small. A four year old. For a moment, Ashley had the most terrible, overwhelming longing for that to be true. She wanted to say. *Oh, Mum, I'm in such trouble.*

Then she looked at her mother's swollen, twisted fingers on the envelope and knew she couldn't do it.

'Oh, Mum, why do you *fret* so much?' Taking the envelope, she pushed it into her pocket. 'I'll go and talk to Vikki after lunch, if you like.'

She picked up the dustpan and brush and went out of the room, just in time. If she hadn't left then, she would have started screaming. It was like balancing on a rope of twisted lies. She kept having to wind in another strand, and another, to keep herself from crashing to the ground.

She opened the larder cupboard and chose a tin of soup for lunch, wondering how long it would all go on. How long would she have to play at being normal, while she waited for more and more horrible messages?

She upended the tin, and the soup flooded out. Tomato soup. Bright scarlet. And the words of the letter flooded into her mind.

You'VE got suCH Red BLOOD . . .

And in that instant, she knew she couldn't just sit around and wait. She couldn't cope if she had to be a victim, looking over her shoulder and inventing excuses to stop her mother finding out. Maybe Eddie's plan would work in the end, but that wasn't enough. She had to do something herself. She had to be in charge.

As she put the soup saucepan on to the gas ring, she saw how to do it. Only one thing made sense. She imagined herself into the scene, as clearly as if she were watching a film. The same little pictures played themselves over and over again. She would take the bones and the letters and the photos, she would go up the road, she would push that door open, and then—

And then—

But it wasn't quite like a film. It was more like a clip that cut out exactly when it had you hooked. If she wanted to know the whole story, she had to step into it and make it real.

By the time she poured the soup into the bowls, her mind was made up. She took the soup into the front room and shared it with Pauline, chatting cheerfully about Janet and Frank and the twins. And about how she was going to visit Vikki after lunch.

But she hadn't got the faintest intention of visiting Vikki. When she'd done the washing up, she went upstairs and piled everything into her school backpack. She was sorry that she couldn't take the scratched drainpipe, or the liver heart, but she had enough for what she wanted to do.

Rattling down the stairs, she stuck her head round the front room door, without going right in, so that her mother wouldn't see the backpack.

'OK, Mum. I'm going round to Vikki's now. If she doesn't know anything about this Cindy stuff, she soon will. You know what she's like. Bye.'

Pauline's mouth opened, but Ashley didn't wait to hear what she was going to say. Waving briskly, she went out and closed the front door firmly behind her.

It was a crisp, cold day. As she went up the road, she was busy pulling her coat round her and pushing her hands into her pockets. The busyness kept her mind full and she didn't need to think at all about the mad, inconceivable thing she was planning. All she had to do was keep walking, until she saw the shop. And all the people inside.

Her audience.

On she went, round the corner and along the Row until she reached Fat Annie's. Then she stopped and looked in at the window.

And her heart dropped like a broken lift.

In her imaginary clip, the shop had been crowded with people, with Fat Annie at the till and the Hyena skulking somewhere near the magazine rack. She had planned to march straight up to Annie and say, *I've got something here that belongs to your son.* Then she was going to tip out everything in the bag, all over the counter.

But Annie wasn't there. There was no one in the shop at all, except the Hyena. He was standing at the till, reading the newspaper. Ashley stared at his doughy face and the way the newspaper shivered in his hands, and she wanted to be a giant, so that she could step on the shop and squash him flat, the way children squash slugs. Her skin shrank round her in revulsion.

He was the one. He'd sent her those horrible messages and the disgusting liver heart. He'd chased her in the dark, and breathed down the phone, into her ear. *Cindy . . . thin bones. . .* He was—

Then he looked up, straight at her. The shock of it was like a blow in the ribs. All he did was smile, but it knocked the breath out of her, so that she couldn't do anything clever or subtle. All she could do was run away or go in to face him. And she'd had enough of running away. That was why she was there.

Taking a deep breath, she pushed the door open.

JANET
We went into McDonald's after we left Pauline, as a treat for the girls. And we'd hardly got home before the phone rang. When Frank answered it, he sighed, the way he does if it's Pauline or Ashley, and passed

212

the phone straight to me. Can't they ever leave you alone? *he was mouthing.*

I thought it was Ashley, of course. I thought something else had happened. I grabbed the phone out of his hand.

'Ashie?' I said. 'Is that you? Is everything all right?'

Only it wasn't Ashley. It was Pauline. And she sounded desperate.

Maybe you can't see what's startling in that. Lots of people would sound desperate all the time, if they had Pauline's life. But she's always been the strong one. She's never given in. Not even when Ben died. Not even when the arthritis got so bad she could hardly stand up, and she had to move into that horrible house, with hardly any money. Frank and I have helped her a lot, of course, but she's never asked us to. Even when we took the girls, it was as if she was doing us a favour and giving us her twins because we couldn't have any children of our own.

There's times I've longed for her to give in. I've seen her so tense, so uptight, that I've said, Go on, Paul. Shout and scream. *Moan a bit. But she never let go, not once. She's always the big sister, being wonderful. And I'm always the little sister who's not quite good enough.*

But that day, it was quite different. Oh, Jan, *she said,* I don't know what to do. I'm so scared. There's something wrong with Ashley and she won't tell me and I don't know what to do about it.

She sounded as if she was going to collapse into tears. I wanted to reach down the phone and hug her.

Oh, Jan, please help me . . . .

That was when I knew I had to tell her.

23

As Ashley walked into the shop, the Hyena looked up, eagerly, and smiled again. It was like watching a wolf smile at her, like watching a tiger. But there was no going back. She was in the shop, and she had to go through with what she'd planned, or things would only get worse.

Do it now, she thought. *Before there's time to be afraid. Now!*

She didn't dare to hesitate. Pulling the pack off her back, she walked straight up to the till and tipped the whole lot out, on to the counter. Letters. Skull. Photographs. They spilled over the grey surface, and the Hyena's hands went out, instinctively, to stop them sliding off.

'Look at them!' Ashley said fiercely. Shouting. 'Do you like them? Are you proud of them?' Her voice rose, but she didn't try to control it. She wanted it to batter him, like a cudgel. 'I'm sick of it! D'you hear? I'm sick of being chased and phoned and persecuted. Why don't you leave me alone?'

The Hyena didn't say anything. He was staring at her, white-faced, with his tongue flicking nervously over his lips.

'Everything you send me, I'm going to show people!' Ashley yelled. 'What d'you think about that? What do you think people will make of this—?'

She pushed the skull at him.

'—or this—?'

She splayed the photographs roughly in her fingers and slammed them down on top of his newspaper.

'—or THIS?'

With both hands, she wrenched the latest note open so that it lay accusingly in front of them both. The newspaper letters danced in front of her eyes.

CinDY

. . . such tHin BONEs . . .

. . . Red BLOOD . . .

. . . suCH Red BLOOD . . . YOU CAN't cARry On Like thaT . . . YouLL Fall

. . . YouLL Fall . . .

. . . YouLL Fall

Youll Fall . . . CinDY . . . CinDY . . . CinDY

The Hyena was utterly stunned, but that only made her angrier. And she could feel her voice giving out, catching in her sore, raw throat. Before it gave way entirely, she picked up the newspaper note and pushed it at him, almost into his face.

'Look!' she shouted. 'LOOK! Are you proud of sending that to me? Did you—?'

She didn't go on, because the Hyena's face changed suddenly. It began to tremble, and he looked desolate. Distraught. *Got you!* thought Ashley. She let the note fall.

'Well?' she said.

When the Hyena spoke, his voice was a whisper. 'No,' he said. 'Oh, no. Please—'

She thought he was going to beg, to ask her not to give him away, and she stood there waiting for him to plead. So that she could refuse.

He was staring down at the note. When his eyes lifted and found her face, they were full of tears.

'Please,' he said. 'I . . . oh please—'

Ashley was flooded with triumph. There was no faking an expression like that. She'd beaten him!

'Please,' he said again. 'It's not true. Say it's not true.'

'What?' The triumph wavered. 'What are you talking about?'

'You're not . . . you're not really Cindy, are you? Please say you're not. You mustn't be Cindy!'

Some things don't make any sense. Some things are too unexpected to take in. All you can do is fix on a tiny part. Ashley looked down at the grey letters and the Hyena's words rattled round her like the clatter of a marching band.

You mustn't be Cindy!

'Why not?' she said, half croaking. 'Why can't I be Cindy?'

'Because . . . because . . . ,

He shrank backwards, but she couldn't bear not to know. Leaning over the counter, she hissed at him.

'What are you talking about? *Why* can't I be Cindy?'

'Because . . . because. . . ,

Flick, flick went his tongue over his lips. He was choking with embarrassment and effort, but Ashley wasn't going to give up.

'*Why* can't I be Cindy?'

The words wrenched themselves out of him. Furiously. So that he was suddenly shouting them into her face.

'Because you're different from the others. Because you're good!'

'What?' Ashley's hands dropped away. She felt numb. 'What are you talking about?'

Behind her, the doorbell clanged and she heard someone walk into the shop. A man's shoes clumped heavily and somehow she managed to step back from the counter to let him buy his cigarettes. As he asked for them, he glanced sideways at her, but she didn't look back and after a moment he went away.

'I thought you weren't like the others,' the Hyena

said, when the door closed again. He was talking in a low, painful mutter now. 'They come in from school and steal things and . . . um . . . make fun of me and treat me—'

He couldn't say it. Ashley didn't want him to say it. She nodded, quickly, to show she knew, and the low, stumbling voice went on.

'I always have to be looking out for shoplifters, and when I catch them, they don't care, they laugh in my face. And mother gets—she hates it. She's full of hate. That's the worst thing, you know. Living with that hate.'

He stopped for a moment. Ashley couldn't move. She couldn't speak. All she could do was wait for him to go on.

When he did, his voice was a little stronger. 'When the graffiti started, up on the wall, and there was this name—'

'Cindy?' Ashley whispered.

The Hyena nodded. 'Mother picked on that. Everything was Cindy. Not just the graffiti. Or the car. Everything. All the time she goes on and on about it, and how awful things are, and how people hate us, and it's always Cindy, Cindy, Cindy. And the only thing that's kept me going—'

Ashley knew what he was going to say. She wished she could stop him, but she couldn't say a word.

'—the only thing that's kept me going was you. Knowing that there was someone who was good and unselfish and . . . and . . . '

Ashley felt as if she'd thrown a brick at Spider Mo. Or jeered at Thick Ed in Special Needs. Or left her mother lying on the floor. She hadn't known, but that was no excuse. And there was no way to explain that his horrible Cindy was just as false as his idea of her as good and unselfish.

'Is that why you've been stalking me?' she said softly. 'Because you thought I was good?'

'What?'

The Hyena looked up at her like a sleepwalker suddenly coming to. And it was only then that Ashley realized what a mistake she'd made.

'You haven't got a clue what I'm talking about, have you?' she said. 'You're not the stalker.'

'What?' he said. 'What do you mean?'

'You can't be the stalker. Because you didn't know I was Cindy. *You don't really knew me at all.*'

DENNIS
I always go into Annie's shop for cigarettes on a Saturday. I'd heard the gossip, of course, but I didn't see why I should stop, just because of that.

So what? *I said, when Penny told me.* Even if it's true, it doesn't make his cigarettes any worse, does it?

But that was before I went in and saw the girl there.

I'd never seen her before, but she can only have been about fourteen. Just like that girl they say he's been stalking. And the moment I walked in I could feel the vibes. There was something going on.

But what could I do? It's so tricky, isn't it? I wanted to say, Does your mother know you're in here? *Or maybe just give her a look, so she knew she ought to get out of the place. But when I tried to catch her eye she wouldn't lift her head, and I was—*

Well, to be honest, I was scared. You can't be too careful these days, if you're a man. Especially when there's gossip like that flying around. If I'd taken an interest in her—the way I knew I should—the next thing you know there might have been people whispering about me on street corners. Crossing the road to keep their children away.

So I went straight out of the shop.

But all the way home I was sick with myself for being a coward. If anything happens, I kept thinking, I'll know it was my fault. If they find that girl's body, I'll know I could have stopped it.

And that's what it's going to come to in the end, isn't it? If they let him go on stalking girls, something terrible's going to happen. I ought to have taken that girl out of the shop and walked her home. And talked a bit of sense into her.

When I got home, I told Penny, and she tried to make me feel better, of course. 'He can't do anything,' she said. 'Not in the shop, with everyone looking on. And if that girl you saw didn't know what people are saying, she'll find out soon enough. Everyone's talking about it. You don't need to worry, Den. It'll be OK.'

She's right, of course. But it keeps coming back to me. And I get a horrible, sick feeling every time I pick up the newspaper or turn on the radio.

There's nothing I can do now, about that girl I saw. But there's one thing I can do—and I will. I'm not going into that shop any more. The sooner they go bust and get out of this neighbourhood, the better it's going to be for everyone.

I'll walk the extra hundred yards and buy my cigarettes in the Spar.

24

'It's not you,' Ashley said, repeating it to make herself take it in. 'You're not the stalker.'

The Hyena blinked across the counter at her. 'What stalker?'

Then he looked down at the things lying in front of him. Slowly his hands moved over the sutures of the skull and his fingers ran down the ugly black lines on the photographs. When he looked up again, his face was bleak.

'You thought. . . that I sent you these?'

Ashley's throat was dry. 'And I thought you were the person who telephoned me. And scratched on the drainpipe under my window. And chased me home in the dark.'

The Hyena's mouth twisted and he shuffled the pictures together. 'But I would never . . . how could you think—?'

Ashley couldn't look at him. 'There were clues, you see. Footprints in my garden, that matched your shoes. And that scarf.'

'I haven't—I don't wear a scarf.'

Ashley leaned forward to contradict him. To say that Annie had recognized the scarf. But just then a woman walked into the shop, to buy a bag of flour. By the time the Hyena had served her, he'd worked out which scarf Ashley meant.

'That scarf—I understand now.' He said it eagerly, wanting to explain. 'My grandfather knitted it. I couldn't possibly—It's not the sort of thing I could wear. But Granny likes to see it. So I keep it in the car. Ready for when I visit her.'

'In the car?' Ashley said slowly. 'You mean—the car that was stolen?'

A picture sharpened in her mind, swimming out of her memory. How could she have forgotten about it? It was perfectly clear now. She could see Sam crashing the Hyena's car into the garages and then jumping out. She saw her running through the Newenthal flats with a long scarf flapping round her neck.

And then she saw her collapsing against the wall of Toronto House, next to Spider Mo. And draping the scarf ceremoniously round Mo's neck.

A yellow scarf, with a black pattern.

'So what did you think?' she said faintly. 'When you got the scarf back?'

'My . . . um . . . my mother said some children had it. I didn't tell her it was in the car. She gets so—' The Hyena avoided Ashley's eyes. 'It's not good when she thinks about the car.'

'So it *was* your scarf I saw,' Ashley said slowly. 'But

I don't know what happened to it after that. That's what I need to find out.'

She left the words hanging in the air and began to scoop the bones and all the other things back into her rucksack. Everything had sharpened suddenly, and she knew what she had to do.

'Ashley—' the Hyena said.

'Yes?' She fastened the pack and looked up. He was twisting his hands together.

'I . . . um . . . I mean . . . you don't still think—?'

His pasty face was pale and mournful, and there were strands of black hair slicked over his balding scalp. It would be easy to make fun of that face. If you didn't know. Ashley rested her backpack on the counter.

'I'm sorry,' she said awkwardly. 'It was a mistake. I wish I hadn't . . . I'm sorry. And . . . for everything else, as well.'

There was so much to apologize for that she didn't know where to start. She picked up the pack again and hooked it over one shoulder.

'But I'm going to find out what's going on.'

'You shouldn't go on your own,' the Hyena said. 'Do you want . . . um . . . shall I shut the shop and come with you?'

Ashley shook her head. 'That's really kind. But it's OK.'

'Well, if you're ever in trouble—'

'Thanks,' Ashley said. 'I'll remember that.'

Then she went out to look for Spider Mo.

It wasn't easy to track down Mo at that time of day. She wasn't an active beggar, like the people who loitered round the shopping centre, tootling on tin whistles. She spent most of her day shuffling round the town centre, from one bench to another. Ashley had seen her a hundred times, on one or another, but that day all the benches were empty.

A couple of old men were slumped on the pavement in one of the doorways along the Row, but Mo wasn't in any of the doorways. And she wasn't in the library.

In the end, Ashley asked the *Big Issue* seller outside HMV. He was there every day. He must know Mo.

'Sure I know her,' he said, but he didn't smile. He looked at Ashley as if she were an earwig. 'Why don't you kids leave her alone? You're always teasing her and knocking her about for no reason. She's harmless if you treat her all right.'

'I know,' Ashley said. 'Really. But I have to ask her something.'

'You're wasting your breath. She'll never remember.'

The man smiled past her and reached over her shoulder to sell a copy of the magazine.

Ashley caught at his sleeve. 'Look! I'm trying to do something good. Please believe me. But I can't do it unless I can find Mo. You don't have to tell me where she is, but please, *please* give me a clue where to look.'

The man dropped the coins into his pocket and looked down at her, examining her face. Then he said gruffly, 'It's pretty cold today. If Mo's got any money, she'll be having a warm drink somewhere. Where it's cheapest.'

'Oh,' Ashley said. 'Thanks.'

She began to walk away, running through the cheap cafés in her mind. Working out how long it would take to visit them all. When she'd taken half a dozen steps, the man called after her.

'Hey!'

She looked back at him, and he grinned.

'Try Popeye's Parlour.'

Ashley grinned back and set off there, through the covered market. When she arrived, she saw that the man was right. Popeye's tea was ten pence cheaper than anywhere else. And even through the steamy window she could see Mo, sitting up at the far end, where it was warmest.

Ashley pushed the door open and strolled up the

café. As she passed Mo, she saw that her cup of tea was almost empty. She bought another and took it back to the table.

'Hi. Would you like this?'

Mo's eyes flicked up at her. Bright black. Suspicious. Then they flicked down to the table again. She ignored the cup of tea, as if it were a trap.

'It's OK,' Ashley said. 'I've bought you some tea because I want to talk to you. It's a trade.'

The eyes looked up again, and stayed on her face. Waiting.

'I want to ask you a question,' Ashley said. 'About . . . about Sam. You do know her?'

'Eddie's Sam?' Mo looked cautious. 'What do you want to know?'

Ashley pushed the tea with one finger, edging it across the table. 'I was with her the other night. A couple of weeks ago. We came through the estate with Joe and Doug. You were sleeping round the back of Toronto House. Remember?'

'I might.' Mo's fingers closed round the teacup. 'So what if I do?'

'And do you remember the scarf Sam gave you? It was yellow.'

Lifting the cup with two hands. Mo took a long swig of the tea. 'It was a good scarf,' she said. 'Warm.'

'And have you still got it?'

Mo was lifting the cup to her mouth. As she drank, she shook her head, and the tea spilled out and trickled down the sides of her chin.

Ashley tried not to look excited. 'Somebody took the scarf away? Who was that?'

She said it as gently as she could, but the effect was disastrous. Mo's face crumpled and she slammed the tea down on to the table, pushing it away so roughly that most of the rest of it spilt.

'No,' she said. 'NO!'

'Please!' Ashley knew she'd blown it, but she couldn't bear to give up. 'Please! You've *got* to tell me where that scarf is!'

'No! No!' Mo started to rock in her chair. 'There wasn't a scarf. I never had a scarf. No! No!'

Out of the corner of her eye, Ashley saw the man behind the counter turn to look at them. He was frowning. In a moment he would come and interfere. She hadn't got long.

'Please, Mo—'

But Mo was picking up her bags now. Gathering them together frantically, to make a getaway. Ashley stood up and leaned forward, trying to stop her. Knocking the bags out of the way.

She was so frantic that she didn't see the *Big Issue* seller come into the café. She didn't notice him at all until he appeared beside her, tall and furious.

'Get out,' he said.

'But I'm not—' Ashley wanted to explain, but he didn't give her a chance. He just glared, scornfully, until she picked up her backpack and sidled out of the shop.

What was she going to do now?

TOM

I thought she was OK. I really thought she was OK, that girl.

When you're out on the Row every day, there aren't many people you don't know. I'd seen that one going backwards and forwards to school, and doing her shopping, and I thought: she's OK. Never bought a magazine, but I reckoned she was pretty short of cash. If she'd come up to me a couple of weeks ago and asked for Mo, I'd have told her without thinking twice.

But then there was all that weird stuff about old GG stalking her.

The story spread like measles. And no wonder. Eddie Beale's boys were all out, making sure everyone got it. And I saw Sam and her mother, too, chatting up the old ladies.

It wasn't obvious, mind. That's not Eddie's style. You wouldn't have noticed anything, if you were out shopping. But I noticed. I could feel the atmosphere on the Row thickening up like soup, and I didn't fancy it.

And when the girl turned up hunting for Mo, I didn't like that either. I told her where to look—didn't take much working out—but I took my coffee break early to keep an eye on things. Mo's a smelly old wreck, but it makes me sick the way people get at her.

And I was right. Of course. When I got to Popeye's, the girl was coming over really heavy. I don't know what she was after, but you could see Mo wasn't going to cough.

I watched until I was sure what was going on. And when I saw Mo start to rock, I went in and sorted out Little Miss Cindy Spray-can. (Oh yes, I know that too. I told you—I don't miss much.) I sent her off with a flea in her ear.

Then I stayed and had my coffee. I was trying to calm Mo down and tell her she was safe, so she wouldn't get flung out into the cold before she'd finished her tea. But I don't think she heard a word I was saying. I couldn't get any sense out of her at all.

Whatever that girl was asking, someone had beaten her to it. They'd really put the frighteners on Mo. She was still shaking when I left her and went back to my pitch. But all she would say was, I didn't tell her. I didn't say a word. *Whatever she knows, there's someone who wants to be sure she won't tell. And I could have a pretty good guess at who it is.*

There's only one person round here who frightens people that much.

25

So what now? Ashley walked back through the market, feeling angry and defeated. She couldn't bear to give up, but she didn't know where else to look.

As she came out on to the Row, Joe appeared beside her. She kept walking and he fell into step, with his big hands hanging loose and his long arms swinging.

'Heard you were looking for Mo,' he said.

Ashley blinked at him. 'Who told you that?'

'People.' Joe leered sideways at her, from under his bobble hat.

Then he hunched his shoulders and started to waddle, so that his whole body looked square. He swayed from side to side, toting imaginary carrier bags.

'Unnph,' he mumbled. 'Got to . . . Friday night . . . it's important . . . '

Ashley didn't smile. 'It's not funny. Mo's not funny.'

Joe's eyes hooded themselves and she felt him take in her expression and the tone of her voice. For the first time, it struck her that he wasn't just a clown. He was a bit of a video camera too. Whatever she did, whatever she said, he could play it back to someone else, later on. *It's not funny. Mo's not funny.* With a toss of the head and a little pinch of the lips, to make it ridiculous.

Imagining his performance, and the eyes that would watch it, she suddenly realized what she had to do next.

'I've got to see Eddie,' she said abruptly. 'Do you know where he is?'

Joe looked wary. 'Maybe. Why do you want him?'

'It's the Hyena—Mr Galt. He's not the stalker after all. I've got to see Eddie and make him tell people.'

Joe pushed his hands into his pockets and stopped. 'Nobody makes Eddie do anything.'

'I'll ask him, then. What difference does it make? There's been a dreadful mistake and we've got to put it right.'

She could feel Joe hesitate, and for one baffled moment she thought he was going to object. Then he shrugged.

'You might find him at Tricia's.'

'Where's that?'

'I'll show you.'

It was getting dark already, but Ashley was determined to do something useful before she went home. She followed Joe along to the far end of the Row, and then right, into Barham Place. Joe led her straight across the square and through a gap in the tall white terrace at the end. Beyond the old houses, there were three small blocks of modern flats, quite different from the Newenthal towers.

Tricia's flat was in the furthest block, at the far end of the walkway. Ashley guessed which flat it was from the white curtains, patterned with red poppies, and the ivy trailing over the balcony. Joe nodded up at it.

'I think Sam's having her hair done,' he muttered. 'So she'll be there, anyway. But she doesn't like being disturbed.'

'I'll risk it,' Ashley said.

They climbed the steps to the first floor and Joe took out a key and let himself in. When he opened the door, Ashley could see right through the flat and into the kitchen at the back.

Sam was sitting by the sink, with a mudpack on her face. Her wet hair was hanging in strings, and Tricia was busy ragging the ends with a pair of scissors. When Joe and Ashley walked in, Sam ignored them.

Tricia spoke without looking round. 'Put the kettle on, Joe. We're both gasping.'

'I've brought Ashley,' Joe said. He picked up the kettle and took it to the tap.

Tricia half-turned and waved the scissors. 'Pull up a chair, Ash. And pretend this mud monster is a total stranger. That way she won't bite you.'

'But I need to talk to her.' Ashley walked round Tricia and knelt down, looking up into Sam's face. 'Can you tell me where Eddie is, Sam? I've got to find him.'

Sam's eyes glittered ice blue in the middle of the mudpack, but her face didn't move. The mask was smooth and undisturbed.

Ashley tried again. 'I've got to tell him that we were wrong. About the stalker.'

Still no reaction. Except, maybe, a catch in Sam's breathing.

'How could you be wrong?' Tricia said. 'There were all those clues.'

'They're fakes!' Ashley said fiercely. 'Someone must have framed him! *He didn't do it!*'

The smooth grey surface of Sam's mask twitched once and then fractured suddenly into thousands of little cracks.

And then the doorbell rang.

'Oh *blast!*' Sam said loudly. The mask crumbled into fragments, and she stood up. 'He's early.'

Ashley thought it was Eddie at the door. Before anyone else could move, she ran down the hall and opened it. But it wasn't Eddie standing there. It was the most beautiful man she had ever seen. His hair was pale and smooth. The grey of his expensive, exquisite suit matched the precise grey of his big, lustrous eyes.

And his shirt was open to the waist, showing a chest like ivory silk.

Ashley was sure she had never met him. *But he recognized her.*

She knew it from the way his eyes snapped and then flicked quickly sideways, avoiding her face. The way he started to smile and then wiped his face clean and blank as he remembered who she was. Somehow, he knew her.

Then Sam called from the kitchen.

'You're too early, Rick! You're a toad!'

Rick.

Ashley's mind lurched, and she heard Tricia's voice, babbling on to Pauline. *Rick's absolutely made Sam's career. You should see some of the pictures he's taken . . .*

Rick was a photographer.

And he was Eddie's friend.

Sickeningly, the pieces started sliding into place. Eddie had a friend who took photographs. And he knew who she was. Sam had had the scarf. And the scarf had turned up just when Eddie said she needed another clue.

Like the phone call that had come just as she got home from Eddie's party. Everything fitted too well.

And it all led back to Eddie in the end.

Furiously, she looked up at the man in the doorway.

'I know who you are!' she said, before she could stop herself. 'You took those horrible photographs!'

The moment she'd said it, she was ice-cold with terror, but there was no going back. Rick reached inside his perfect jacket and took out a tiny mobile phone. It was the same ivory white as his long, beautiful hands. Still watching Ashley, he tapped in a string of numbers and then raised the phone to his ear, holding it a fraction of an inch away, so that it didn't touch his skin.

'Eddie,' he said, 'I'd come round to Sam's if I were you. And bring a *huge* cork. The dam's struck a leak.'

RICK

It was bound to happen, of course. Eddie can't strong-arm the whole world into silence, even if he does think it's his own private circus. Sometimes the tightrope walker breaks out. And this one was way along her own wire. I'd never seen anyone so up and so tight. Believe me, the whole big top was juddering.

Sam came out of the kitchen with her hair wet and her face scrubbed clean. That little pulse was beating in her throat, the way it does when she's driving too fast, or posing on top of a church steeple. She caught at the girl's arm and I almost fainted. I was terrified there was going to be some kind of skirmish.

But not a bit of it. Little Miss Tightrope Walker sat

down in one of Tricia's appalling repro Louis XV chairs. Virtually chained herself to it. Darling, *I wanted to say,* no one has the faintest desire to lay a finger on you. We'll leave that to Eddie. *But she wouldn't have heard. She was watching that door like a cat at a mousehole. She actually wanted him to come.*

It was rather amusing, in a grim way.

When the bell rang she jumped up and faced the door, like a gladiator, but she didn't open it. Joe was left to play doorman. The girl stood on the other side of the hall, trembling like a guitar string.

Well, my darling, *I thought,* we all learn by making mistakes. I bleed for you, I really do. But I think I'm going to enjoy this.

I was looking forward to seeing what Eddie pulled out of the hat. To keep her in line.

239

26

Two heavies came through the door first. Big men in jeans and T-shirts. They stepped sideways, framing the entrance, and Eddie came after them, with his eyes on Ashley.

She was beyond thinking. Her mind had flashed like quicksilver to an answer she had never expected. All she could do was speak it out, and the words erupted, the moment she saw Eddie's face.

'You tricked me! The stalker was you! You sent people to take photographs, and push things through my door, and you tried to make me think it was Mr Galt!'

Eddie stepped into the hall, neat as a cat, and shut the door behind him. 'Well done,' he said. 'You worked it out. It took you long enough.'

'But why?' Ashley said. 'What's the point?'

'Maybe it was just for fun.' Eddie leaned back against the door. 'It's a good laugh, isn't it?'

If he'd tried to pretend, Ashley could have coped. If he'd told her she was mad, she would have known where she was. His calmness threw her right off balance.

Behind her back, she could hear Tricia whispering

to Sam. The two heavies were smirking, and she could see Rick glancing over at Eddie, and Joe tracing shapes on the floor with his toe. They all knew more about what was going on than she did. She could feel the knowledge all round her, just out of reach. It was like being in a theatre before the play, watching muffled shapes move behind the curtains.

Her eyes darted round from face to face, trying to pick up some extra clue. But the only person who looked back at her was Eddie.

'What did you think was going on?' he said scornfully. 'Did you think I was going to all that trouble just to save you from a few loony letters?'

'I thought . . . you were being kind,' Ashley said slowly. 'People said—'

'Ye-es?' He tilted his head on one side, watching her. Amused.

Ashley spun round to Tricia. 'You told my mum he helped people!'

'He does,' Tricia said easily. 'Don't take any notice of what he says. He's got to talk tough, to keep people in order, but he's got a heart of gold. Look how he rescued Joe from that horrible Vince.' She ruffled Joe's hair and opened the kitchen door. 'I'm not listening to this stuff. When you've sorted it out, come through and have a drink.'

She went in and shut the door behind her. Very

softly, under her breath, Sam said, 'That's Mum all over. Get out when things turn nasty.'

'And why not?' Joe said. His hand went up to his head, but it wasn't his own hair he was patting. It was Tricia's blonde candyfloss. 'Why do people want to look at the nasty things? What I say is—'

He wriggled his shoulders girlishly and his voice got shriller, going up a couple of notches, like a tape getting faster.

'—what I say is if you don't look on the bright side, you might as well be d—'

'Joe.'

Eddie's voice sliced through the chatter. Joe stopped halfway through the word, with his mouth open and his two eyes wide, like dark moons.

'Shut it,' Eddie said.

Slowly Joe's big mouth closed, and he folded up like an umbrella, squatting on the floor with his sharp knees under his chin.

'That's better,' Eddie said. He flicked his fingers at Sam. 'Go and tell Tricia we'll be through in a minute. She can get out some beers.'

Sam looked at him. Then she turned abruptly and went into the kitchen. Eddie nodded a signal and Joe leaped up and closed the door behind her.

'You see?' Eddie murmured. He glanced across at Ashley. 'Even Sam does what I say. It's the only way to be. Keep your mouth shut and your eyes closed. There are things it's better not to think about.'

'I can't do that,' Ashley said stubbornly. 'Not now I know what you're up to. You're trying to wreck Annie's shop, aren't you?'

Eddie jerked upright and took a step towards her. Suddenly, he pushed his face at her, and his eyes were like steel. 'Say that outside this flat, and you'll be sorry.'

'What do you mean?' Ashley edged backwards.

'It's slander, that's what I mean. You can't prove anything. The first whisper about stalking, or plotting against Fat Galt, and you're in trouble. And so's your mother.'

'But you can't—'

'You think I haven't got any solicitors?' Eddie sat back and looked at her, scornfully. 'You don't have a clue, do you? Look around. I've got Rick to take my photographs. Sam and Joe to keep me amused. Tricia to do home cooking if I fancy it. And . . . these.' He flicked his fingers at the men by the door. 'There's someone of mine in every street round here. In every pub and every block of flats. I'm the ringmaster and they all jump when I crack the whip.'

He looked round the hall, daring the others to answer. The heavies were expressionless, but Rick

243

raised a rueful eyebrow and Joe dropped his head on to his knees.

Eddie laughed softly. 'I give them what they want. That's why they stick with me. And you're the same.'

'No I'm not.' Ashley clenched her fists. 'You can't buy me with a secondhand DVD player.

'Don't be silly,' Eddie said. He leaned sideways and snapped his fingers at Rick. 'Show her the photographs.'

Rick reached inside his jacket and took out a pale blue envelope. Suddenly, danger glittered in the air. The heavies leaned forward to see what was in the envelope, and Joe lifted his head and glanced at Ashley.

Rick slid a long finger under the flap. There were ten or fifteen photographs in the envelope and he fanned them out under Ashley's nose. She looked down, expecting to see more ugly pictures of herself.

But she was nowhere, and the pictures were beautiful. They showed two women laughing in an autumn wood. Their faces glowed among the scarlet and crimson and gold of the leaves.

Tricia and—

Rick pushed the pictures at Ashley, flicking through them so that Tricia seemed to rise and dance under the trees. In the last couple of pictures, the other woman was on her feet too, standing with her arms spread wide and her head flung back. She was laughing like a teenager.

'Mum,' Ashley said.

'That day they went out to look at the leaves.' Rick peered down at the pictures. 'Not bad, are they? Considering I had to get them without being seen.'

'Show her the other one,' Eddie said sharply. 'The one you took before.'

Ashley guessed what kind of picture he was talking about. But she didn't see how Rick could have taken one, until he pulled it out of the envelope and showed her. Then she caught her breath.

'That's our house!'

He must have been outside, looking in through the window. The picture showed the front room at its worst, with heaps of dirty clothes all over the floor. In the foreground was Pauline, sitting up in bed. She was grey-faced and her long hair—the old, untended hair—trailed into her coffee.

Ashley glared. 'You were spying!'

'Darling, it was dreadful!' Rick pulled a pathetic face. 'I couldn't get a really good shot. It's a pity when the others came out so well.'

'Never mind,' Eddie said smoothly. 'You'll be able to take a replacement. The lady's going to look like that again, when Tricia gives up visiting.'

Ashley stared down at the horrible, depressing picture. 'And suppose Tricia doesn't stop?'

Eddie pulled a face at her. Wide-eyed and innocent. 'Your mother won't want her to come, will she? Not when she knows it was all done out of pity. And Tricia thinks she's a boring old cow.'

'It's not true,' Ashley said. Fighting off the image of her mother hearing those words and shrinking back into her old, miserable self. Shrinking back too far for anyone to reach her. 'It's not true! Tricia wouldn't—'

'Tricia,' said Eddie, 'will do whatever I tell her to. She's no fool.'

'But they're friends! Tricia likes Mum! Ask Sam—'

'Sam?' said Eddie. Very softly. *'Sam?* You think *she's* going to argue with me?' His mouth started to twitch and he looked across at Joe, tilting his head slightly.

It was a signal. For a second, Ashley thought Joe was going to disobey. Then Eddie jerked a finger at him and he bounded up, long-legged and defiant, with his hands bunched. He held one fist under Eddie's nose and shook it.

'You don't tell *me* what to do! Maybe you can push all the others around, but not me. We're equals, aren't we, Eddie Beale?'

He had it, exactly. Even the way Sam stood, with her feet wide apart and one hip pushed forward, aggressively. Ashley saw him dissolving, in front of her eyes, giving way to an image of Sam, as crude and powerful as a cartoon.

Eddie's finger beckoned, slowly. It was Joe he drew towards him, but it wasn't Joe that the watchers saw. Not Joe who moved forward, responding to that power, crumpling to the ground as Eddie pointed.

It was like seeing Sam on her knees in front of the dusty toes of Eddie's shoes. Joe leaned over them and stretched out his tongue, pretending to lick away the dust. And all the time he was waving his fist in the air, in a pantomime of independence.

No one else moved. No one made a sound.

'He's a real scream,' Eddie said, into the silence. 'Isn't he?' He glanced round sharply at the men by the door. 'Shaun? Dave?'

The men sniggered obediently and Eddie looked back at Rick and Ashley. Rick's face twisted into a sickening grin, but there was no smile in his eyes. Ashley turned her head away.

Eddie wasn't going to let her escape. He stepped sideways, so that she had to look at him. 'What's wrong with you? Got no sense of humour?'

'I—' Her voice caught in her throat.

'Everyone else thinks it's hilarious,' Eddie said smoothly. His mouth twitched again, and he looked past her, over her shoulder. *'Everyone.'*

Ashley spun round. The kitchen door was open.

Sam was standing there, with a four-pack of lager in one hand. Beyond her was Tricia, breaking open a bag of crisps. Ashley could tell by their faces that they had seen Joe's imitation too.

'Laugh!' Eddie snapped.

There was a hair's-breadth pause, and then Tricia gave a forced, nervous cackle. When Ashley turned away, she met Eddie's eyes.

'You see?' he murmured. 'Tricia knows it's best to play things my way. If you don't, you might get—hurt.'

Ashley couldn't speak. She felt the air crowding in and the walls threatening her. Eddie nodded across at Rick.

'Give her the pictures.'

Rick pushed them into her hand, closing her fingers round them so that they didn't fall. She looked down and saw Pauline's grey face staring back at her.

'Think it over,' Eddie said. 'And remember, it's not going to help your mother if anything happens to you.'

They all stood and watched her as she stumbled across the hall and opened the front door. She stepped outside and glanced back once, as she pulled the door shut behind her. The last thing she saw in the flat was Sam's face. Sam's unreadable, ice-blue stare, following her as she walked away.

SHAUN

The funny thing was—Sam didn't laugh.

The girl went off down the stairs and we all stood there, listening to her feet.

'She'll come round,' Eddie said. 'When she's had time to think it over. Won't she, Sam?'

And he lifted his head, in that way he has. Looking for an answer. But Sam didn't say a word. She stood in the kitchen doorway with the lager hanging from her hand, and you couldn't tell what the hell she was thinking.

Usually, she has everything in her face. In those photos Rick takes, you can see exactly what she's thinking, *Out of my way, worm!* and *Get your hands off my leathers! Stuff like that. It's great.*

But just then there was nothing. She stared back at Eddie and she never answered him at all.

It was Joe who jumped up—for no reason, as far as I could see. He charged down the hall into his bedroom and shut the door. Slammed it. It could have been a nasty moment, but Tricia came out with the crisps and we all had a beer and went in to watch the match.

27

Ashley didn't know what to do, so she went home. There was nowhere else to go.

She walked round the block for ten minutes, until her face was under control. Then she plastered a smile on it and let herself in.

'Hi, Mum. Sorry I was so long.' She strode into the front room. 'You know what it's like when Vikki and I get talking.' She could hear her voice sounding shrill and brittle and she smiled harder.

Pauline was sitting at the table, with a bag of sprouts in front of her, peeling them and dropping them into a bowl. She looked up, and her hands stopped moving, but she didn't say a word.

'I asked Vikki about that Cindy letter.' Ashley laughed brightly. 'But she hadn't got a clue who could have sent it—'

There was something unnerving about Pauline's expression. She was just letting the words wash over her, as if they had no importance.

Ashley faltered. 'Are you all right?'

Pauline pulled another leaf off the sprout she was holding. 'Ash, you don't have to keep on fooling me. I know.'

Ashley's heart lurched. 'What are you talking about?'

'I phoned Janet. She said the intruder was Mr Galt, and he's been stalking you for weeks. Why didn't you tell me?'

Ashley's brain churned. 'I . . . I didn't want to worry you.'

'Don't you think I was worried anyway?' Pauline picked at the sprout again. I *knew* there was something wrong.'

It was a sickening, black joke. Ashley felt the whole, tangled story swirl around her. *True/false, true/false, true/false.* She'd struggled to stop Pauline finding out about the stalker and, now she did know, there was something worse to hide. The real truth.

And the threats.

Eddie's voice echoed in her mind. *Keep your mouth shut and your eyes closed. There are things it's better not to think about. It's the best way, if you want a quiet life. If you want me to look after things.* She had to get away and pull herself together.

'I'll go and make some tea,' she muttered. 'Do you want a cup?'

Pauline put the sprout down. 'No, I don't!' she said sharply. 'I want you to talk to me.'

'We can talk with the tea,' Ashley said briskly. 'I won't be long.'

She was almost through the door, when Pauline said, 'Don't go.'

It was quite soft. Ashley could have pretended not to hear, and carried on down the hall. But there was a firmness in Pauline's voice that made her stop. She turned round.

'What's hurting you?' Pauline said. Very gently.

Ashley felt the answer inside her like a lump of stone. She seemed to have been carrying it round all her life. Keeping it inside because the world would collapse around her if she ever let it out.

Pauline pulled herself on to her feet and lurched slowly across the room towards her, holding on to the furniture. When she stopped, they were near enough to touch.

'Tell me,' she said.

How can I? Ashley thought. She wanted to pour it all out. She wanted to fling herself into her mother's arms and yell and scream. But if she tried, both of them would fall over. And there was no one else to pull them up.

But even while she was remembering all that, she heard her own voice. Heard the lump of stone rolling out of her mouth.

'I don't know what to do. I'm in a mess and I just . . . can't *manage!*'

Then the words caught in her throat and choked

her, and Pauline opened her arms. Ashley went into them and, as they closed round her, the two of them tottered and fell over, just as she'd known they would, crumpling into an untidy, undignified heap on the floor. But Pauline just laughed and sat up, keeping her arm tightly round Ashley's shoulders.

'Now tell me,' she said.

And Ashley did tell her, sitting there on the carpet. She told her everything, without trying to tidy it up or miss out the parts that would hurt. Every single thing, right from the beginning.

When she finished, Pauline sat very still, stroking her hand.

'Do you know something?' she said. 'That's the first time you've asked me for help, since you were seven.'

'Only because you've had enough to put up with. And because—'

'Because you had to cope.' Pauline nodded. 'I know. And you were afraid of what would happen if you didn't. It's frightening, isn't it? Well, now we've landed on the floor, and there's nowhere else to go.' She straightened her shoulders. ' So how can we tell people that Mr Galt is innocent?'

'Go to the police?' Ashley said.

'We haven't got any evidence. We have to sort it out ourselves.'

'But Eddie won't *let* us! I told you!'

'He can't stop us if we do it fast enough. We need to tell hundreds of people at once. Couldn't we call a meeting?'

Ashley pulled a face.

'We must do something!' Pauline said desperately. 'What about posters?'

Another poster? The empty shops were covered in them. People just didn't bother to read things like that.

Unless . . . A plan exploded suddenly in Ashley's brain, like fireworks in the sky. *Yes! That was how to get words across*! But would her mother—?

Pauline looked at her sharply. 'You've thought of something.'

Ashley hesitated, tempted to keep her idea secret. To fob Pauline off with a half-truth and pretend she was going to put up useless posters. She could do that—

But she wasn't going to. Not any more.

'Yes, I have thought of something,' she said steadily. 'It means climbing on to that roof again. But I won't do it unless you say it's all right.'

Pauline looked down at her fingers. 'Will it work?'

'I think so. Especially if Mr Galt helps me.'

Pauline took a deep breath. 'You're sure about him, are you, Ashie? You're sure he's not—'

'Certain,' Ashley said.

There was a long silence. Very slowly, Pauline nodded. 'You'd better phone him then, hadn't you? But take me into the kitchen first. I don't want to know the details.'

The Hyena wasn't easy to persuade. 'It's so . . . so dangerous,' he kept saying.

'But it'll work,' Ashley said. 'Won't it?'

'I . . . um . . . well, yes. I suppose so. But if you fall—'

'I *won't* fall. I've done it before.'

'But what about your mother?'

'She—' *What?* thought Ashley. Then the words came, and she knew they were true. 'Mum doesn't like it either, but she trusts me. She says yes.'

The Hyena swallowed noisily. 'Well, if she thinks ... I suppose I can . . . um—'

When Ashley put the phone down, she found she was shaking.

She and Pauline both tried to sleep, but neither of them succeeded. At a quarter to two, Ashley picked up her backpack, padded downstairs and stuck her head round the front room door. Pauline's bedside light was on, and she was sitting up, waiting.

'I'm going now,' Ashley said.

'You will. . . be careful?'

'Yes. I promise.' Ashley slipped down the hall and out of the kitchen door. The grass in the back garden crunched frostily under her feet, and her fingers left black, melted patches on the fence.

Spider Mo was round at the side of Mrs Macdonald's, curled up among the dustbins. Ashley almost fell over her and Mo grunted and sat up for a second. There was a glint of light as she opened her eyes.

'Knock it off, Eddie,' she muttered. Then she slumped back against the dustbins and started snoring.

Out on the pavement, the litter was edged with frost, and the puddles had a rim of ice. Ashley walked lightly, trying to visualize what she was going to do.

The Hyena was standing at the end of the alley, watching out anxiously for her. He started whispering as soon as she was close enough to hear.

'I've been . . . um . . . looking at the roof. It's too dangerous. You can't possibly—' He bit at his lip. 'You really *can't*. Not in this weather. Let me—'

Ashley almost laughed, remembering how miserable he'd looked when he was up there painting the wall.

'I'll be fine. I've done it twice already, remember. But it would be good if you kept a lookout.'

For a second, she thought he wasn't going to let her into the yard. Then he stepped aside and she went through and took hold of the drainpipe.

'Whistle if you see anyone around,' she whispered. 'What can you whistle?'

'Er . . . "God Save the Queen"?'

'Fine.' Ashley grinned at him and started to climb.

When she reached the top of the extension roof, she looked down and saw the pale shape of his face, tipped up to watch her. Then he turned away and walked out of the yard, heading for the Row.

Ashley forgot about him, and concentrated on the roof in front of her. Thank goodness the Cavalieris hadn't insulated their loft. The frost had melted. Putting one foot on the windowsill, she hauled herself up.

When she reached the wall, she stopped, working out exactly what she was going to do with the space. This was the most important piece of writing she'd ever done and she had to make sure it could be read easily from down in the street. For several minutes she stood still, sizing up the space and working out how best to use it. Then her fingers started to get cold, and she pulled out the first can and began.

The letters spread across the wide white space.

STALKING
MONDAY 4PM
BE HERE !

When she had shaded them—from light, bright
yellow at the top, to heavy crimson at the bottom—
she added one more word.

CINDY.

No little drops of blood this time. Instead, she trailed
a string of flowers from the crimson tail of the Y. Then
she pushed the top on to her spray-can and started
back to the ground.

There was not a sound. Not a movement in the air.
She didn't even know where the Hyena was. As she
held on to the gutter, lowering one leg towards the
window, she felt like the only person in the world.
Settling her foot on the windowsill, she lowered the
other one to join it and then bent down, to grip the
windowframe.

And she found herself staring into a huge white
face, peering at her between the curtains.

Her foot slipped, scrabbling uselessly at the edge of
the windowsill, and she felt the wood crack under her
and give way. She clutched at the windowframe, but
her fingers couldn't find a hold and she went scraping
down the wall of the building.

She didn't stop until her feet thudded on to
the extension roof. For an instant she was right off

balance, and she thought she was going to fall. Then she landed on her knees and threw herself towards the drainpipe, sliding down so fast that she burnt her hands. She was across the yard and almost through the gate when the Hyena appeared.

'What's the matter?' he whispered. 'I saw you coming down—'

Ashley caught at his arm. 'I've got to get away. There was a face. Tony Cavalieri—'

She pointed up at the window, but the curtains had fallen together again.

'It's all right,' the Hyena said. 'Tony's . . . um . . . he can't do anything, you know. But you don't have to . . . let me make sure you get home all right.'

MRS CAVALIERI

Usually I sleep. With a life like mine, you sleep when your head hits the pillow. Flat out until the morning. But that night I woke up just after two o'clock.

There were movements. Someone was shuffling about at the back of the house.

I didn't waste time with trying to wake Pete—he'll have problems with the Last Trumpet. I slipped out of my bed and went to see.

And there was Tony, down at the end of the landing.

My heart! I thought it was a ghost. I was thinking

he'd never move out of that room of his. Never again. It was two years he'd been lying there, or sitting in the chair, and I'd watched him bloating up, till—if you're a mother you'll know how I felt. If I didn't go to sleep so fast, I'd cry into my pillow every night.

But now there he was, in his wheelchair, gazing out of the back window. I was afraid to disturb him.

But he heard me and he spun the chair round. 'Here!' he said.

That's one thing he's never lost, my Tony. He's always been good at giving orders. I went down the landing and he pointed through the window.

'Take a look. Tell me what you see.'

I just caught a glimpse of them, before they disappeared down Railway Street. The last people you'd expect to see in the middle of the night.

It was Geoffrey from next door, with the girl there's been all the fuss about.

Mind you, I never believed it. All that stuff about stalking. Eddie's been out to get Annie ever since she refused to pay him off. There was bound to be trouble there sooner or later. There's always trouble if you cross Eddie.

We ought to know.

When Annie stopped paying, I told her, 'You're in for trouble.' But all she said was, 'I'll give him trouble! The first time my window's broken, or I'm burgled—

he's had it. I'm straight round to the police and I'm camping there until they take him in.'

She should have known he wouldn't be so obvious. If Eddie wants to fix someone, he likes it to be a surprise. And when those stories started, about Geoffrey and the stalking, I said to Pete, 'Well. We know who's behind that!'

But the girl, with Geoffrey—now that was something different. I didn't know what that meant.

'So what's going on?' Tony said.

Oh, my heart again! That was the first question he'd asked since the fight. The first time he'd shown any interest in anything.

'It's a long story,' I said.

'So? We've got all night.'

28

The writing was on the wall—but Eddie wasn't going to ignore it. Ashley knew he would try and find out what was going on. But she didn't guess how.

Not until Sunday afternoon.

She and Pauline were watching the television when the phone rang. Ashley jumped and snatched up the receiver.

Before she could say a word, Vikki started in.

'Ash, what are you up to? What's all this stuff about Monday at four o'clock?'

'You saw the wall?' Ashley said.

'Did I see it! I nearly fainted! And the minute I got home. Matt rang and said, "What's going on?" Mum said he'd rung three times already. What are you going to do?'

'I—' Ashley was about to blurt it all out. The words were already formed in her mind. But something, some extra alertness, kept Vikki's words sounding in her head. *Mum said he'd rung three times already.* That was weird. 'Why is Matt so interested in what I'm doing?' she said.

'Of course he's interested!' Vikki shrieked. 'He's your friend. And anyway, Ginger and Phil were on at him about it. Not that he'd tell them, of course, but—'

Ashley didn't hear the rest of what she said. Her brain was working at double speed. So that was how Eddie knew so much about her. Vikki told Matt, and Matt told his big sister Ginger.

Who was going out with Phil Carson.

Eddie's Phil.

Ashley closed her eyes. It was one thing to work out how your secrets leaked away. It was quite different to know for sure. Well, if Eddie wanted information about what she was up to, he was going to get it.

'I'm going to make an announcement,' she said, picking her words. 'From up on the roof.'

She was sharply aware of Pauline, on the other side of the room.

Vikki gave a funny little squeak. 'The roof of the chippie?'

'Don't tell anyone,' Ashley said quickly. Thinking, *I'm sorry, Vik. I haven't told you a lie, but you'll think I did.*

'Of course I won't tell anyone!' Vikki was indignant. 'But what are you going to say?'

'Why don't you turn up and see? I don't want to spoil the surprise. Bye.' Ashley put the phone down and looked across the room at Pauline. 'Vikki,' she said. 'That's how Eddie knew I was Cindy. Because Vikki gossips.'

Pauline was looking pale. 'And you want her to gossip now?'

'She'd better!' Ashley said fiercely. 'I want Eddie to think I'm going up on the roof of the chippie. So he doesn't find me.'

That was easy to say, but it needed planning. She was going up on the cinema roof instead, and that was right opposite the chippie. She had to get there without being seen, by anyone. Eddie's words kept running over and over in her mind.

There's someone of mine in every street round here. In every pub and every block of flats. I'm the ringmaster and they all jump when I crack the whip.

The only way to be sure of beating him was to get up early. Ashley set her alarm for five o'clock in the morning. By quarter-past five she was down, carrying her backpack.

When she looked into the front room, Pauline pushed herself up on one elbow. Her eyes were dark from lack of sleep.

'Is this it?'

Ashley nodded.

'Do you have to go so early? It's cold out there.'

'I've got lots of clothes. And things to eat. Don't worry.'

'Don't *worry?*' Pauline dredged up a grin from somewhere. 'What do you want? A miracle?'

'It's OK,' Ashley said gently. 'There'll be hundreds of people there. Eddie won't be able to do a thing. I'll be back around half past four, to tell you all about it.' She waved and let herself out into the street, walking briskly up towards the Row.

As she reached the traffic lights, she glanced quickly over her shoulder. Fat Annie's was closed, but the lights were on, and she could see the Hyena, behind the security shutters. He raised a hand, wishing her luck, and she nodded back at him. Wondering if Annie had given him a bad time when he refused to paint the wall again.

Trying not to hurry, she walked down the side of the cinema, into the car park. It was deserted, but the security lights were very bright, lighting up the scrawled graffiti on the back wall. There were a couple of her own there and she was proud of them, but just now she wished she'd left the place alone. The manager had fought back, with long revolving spikes round all the drainpipes, and strands of barbed wire along the gutters. She hoped her extra piece of blanket would be thick enough to cope.

There was only one place where she could climb without being seen from Toronto House, and the wire was thickest there. She scratched her legs three times on the way up and one of the scratches wouldn't stop bleeding. When she reached the roof, she had to wind the tattered blanket round it and wait for it to stop.

By then, the sky was getting light and the Row was noisier. She crawled forward, along the flat roof, until she was hidden by the top of the ventilation shaft. Then she unpacked the warm clothes from her rucksack and pulled them on. After that, there was nothing to do except lie flat and wait. It was a long, cold, boring day.

At midday, she ate her sandwiches and drank a bottle of water. The cinema was open now, and she didn't dare to move much, in case someone heard her. She flexed her muscles carefully, going over and over what she meant to say at four o'clock and checking the time every ten minutes or so. Four o'clock was very slow in coming, and there were lots of panicky thoughts to fight off.

What would she do if someone found her before she was ready? What if no one came to listen? And if people did come, what would she do after she'd spoken? She tried to make plans, but the answers were just stories, spun in her head. There was nothing real except the flat roof and the waiting.

At half-past three, she began to hear a buzz from down in the Row. Cautiously, she wriggled forward across the roof. In front of her, the huge false front of the cinema reared up in an elaborate curving wall. In the centre, it was three times as tall as she was, but at the sides it swept down to make a low parapet. She lifted her head just high enough to see over it.

Even though no one was back from school yet, the pavements were full of people loitering about and looking in shop windows. There was no mistaking why they were there. The way they kept looking at their watches gave it away and Ashley felt her heart beating harder. It was real. It was going to happen.

And there was no sign of Eddie.

At a quarter to four, the kids began to arrive from school, and the buzz grew louder. She peeped again, and saw people jostling each other off the edges of the pavement. There was a crowd of boys peering in at Fat Annie's window and jeering at the Hyena. Lisa was there too, and so were Vikki and Matt, with their arms around each other.

But still she couldn't see Eddie. Or any of his friends that she knew.

Most people had their backs to her. They were looking up at the painted wall, as if they expected someone—or something—to appear up there. It would take a very loud shout to turn them round.

Ashley began to clear her throat, ready to stand up and yell over the parapet.

Was it going to be that easy? Was she going to do it without Eddie trying to stop her?

She was just beginning to believe that, when there was a burst of sound, coming from Shepherds Corner, so loud that it drowned the muttering from below. Circus music filled the air, as if the Row was about to fill up with lions and elephants, with white-faced clowns, in baggy trousers, and girls in sequins swinging high above the ground.

And now, before your very eyes . . .

Sheltering behind the parapet, Ashley stood up and looked along the Row. There was a procession approaching, moving slowly down the middle of the road.

Eddie was in front, driving a car with a loudspeaker strapped to the roof. He had the window down, and as he drove he was waving to people and calling their names.

Behind him, pulling another car on ropes, were Phil and Doug and the two heavies who had been in Tricia's flat. They were tugging at the ropes and making a performance of it. Every few yards, they stopped to pose and flex their muscles.

Sam was on top of the car, sitting on the roof. Her legs were curled under her and she was wearing one of her tiny, glittering dresses. Ashley could see boys waving and whistling, but she stared away over their heads, looking grand and remote.

Last of all came Joe. He was marching along behind Sam's car, grinning left and right and juggling four sticks with the ends wrapped in cloth, like the torch Sam had used at the party.

Eddie stopped outside Fat Annie's, still in the middle of the road, and got out of his car, leaving the music blaring. The men behind him dropped their ropes and Sam stretched and stood up on the roof of her car.

By now, the sound of the music was accompanied by furious hooting from the trapped cars at the ends of the Row. Eddie ignored those. He stepped back, raising his arms to Sam, and the crowd surged forward to see what was going to happen.

It was impossible to hear anything, but Sam didn't need to speak. She bent down and took a bottle from Phil. Then she waited. Joe handed one of his torches to Doug, and Ashley saw the flicker of a cigarette lighter, and the flare as the cloth caught fire.

She looked at her watch. It was exactly four o'clock. What was she going to do? Everyone in the crowd was watching Sam, and she had no way of attracting people's attention. No one was going to hear her announcement.

She tried anyway. Stepping sideways, so that she was clearly visible above the lowest part of the parapet, she opened her mouth and yelled at the very top of her voice.

'Hey, everyone! Look up here!'

It was useless. Even while she was yelling, she could feel the wall of sound from below, swallowing her words and swamping her voice. The music battered her back and as far as the crowd was concerned she was invisible. Everyone was watching Sam as she raised the bottle to her lips.

Taking a swig from it, she lifted the lighted torch, paused dramatically, and then breathed out, sending a jet of flame down the road, right over Joe's head. Ashley couldn't hear the cheers, but she saw people clapping and yelling and she thought. *He's done it. He's beaten me.* As Sam raised the bottle again, she turned her head away in despair.

That was when she saw the huge, pale face across the road. Tony Cavalieri was staring at her, from the upstairs window of the chippie.

TONY CAVALIERI
Yeah, of course I spotted her. As soon as I heard the procession and wheeled myself to the window. I know how Eddie works, you see. If he comes down the road with a circus like that—all that music, and Sam doing

her fire-eating bit—it's like he's saying Look at this! Look over here!

And that means he's probably hiding something. Trying to distract you from looking somewhere else.

So I ignored his stuff and concentrated on spotting the other thing. And the moment I saw that girl up on the cinema—well, it was obvious. When I saw her in the night, she must have been painting that notice on the wall, and now she was there to deliver. But Eddie had stuck his knife in.

No need to tell me about all that.

The thing you've got to understand about Eddie is, everything he does is for real. When we both had gangs, I got a kick out of trying to con him. It was all part of the game, and I thought he felt that way too— until the day when I finally did con him. That night, when I got home, there were six heavies waiting in the back yard.

No one could ever pin it on Eddie, but he's the one who put me in this chair. In the beginning, I used to sit and scream because of not being able to get back at him. I wanted to open the window and yell at the whole world, It was Eddie Beale! But there wasn't any way to make people listen. So when I saw that girl on the cinema, shouting her head off without being heard, it was like seeing myself.

Only this time—at last—there was something I

could do to make it happen. I saw her up there, and I thought, You can do it for me, sweetheart. I didn't know what she had to say, of course, but I'd seen her with Geoff and that was good enough. Eddie's been out to smash Geoff and Annie's shop, ever since Annie stopped paying him off.

If that girl was on Geoff's side, I was going to see she got a hearing. And—after all those years of waiting—it was easy. I didn't need a gang. Or legs. All I had to do was open my window as wide as it would go, and push.

29

Tony Cavalieri grinned and raised his hand. Ashley was still working out what he meant when he started to push the television on to the windowsill.

It was a small portable television, and it must have been standing on a shelf by the window. For a second it tottered on the sill. Then it tipped forward and fell, crashing on to the pavement in front of the chippie. The pavement was empty, because people there had crowded forward, towards Sam's car, but the crash was only inches away from some of them. They turned round furiously as the broken glass flew about, and shouted up at the window.

Tony shouted back in a frenzy, turning bright red and waving his fist. Ashley couldn't hear what he was saying—no one could have heard—but there was no mistaking what he meant. He was gesturing across the road with his whole body, waving his fist and leaning out of the window to make people turn the other way and look across the road.

At Ashley.

One by one, they did turn, until everyone was staring up at her. She saw Vikki and Matt. Lisa. Mrs Macdonald. People she had known all her life and total strangers. Sam spun round on the roof of the car and Joe put down his unlit torches. Suddenly, she was on stage, with people waiting to see what she was going to do.

But what could she do? Her only plan had been to bellow out a message, but that was out of the question.

She turned towards Eddie, with some crazy notion of pointing at him and hoping that people would guess what she meant. But the moment she saw him, the idea shrivelled. He was watching her with a faint, amused smile, enjoying her dilemma.

Slowly, he cocked one eyebrow, giving her that long, long stare that meant. *So? What are you going to do then? What's your trick?*

It was a taunt. He was daring her to put on a show. Well, if he wanted a performance, she was going to give him one. Defiantly, she stepped up on to the parapet.

Immediately, she felt the stillness. The loudspeaker went on blaring away, but the crowd stopped moving. Looking down, Ashley saw Lisa's eyes open wider and Vikki clutch at Matt's arm. Everyone was waiting to see what would happen.

The only person who moved was the Hyena. He came suddenly out of the shop and started pushing forward, past Vikki and Matt. His face was chalk white as he looked up.

From where Ashley stood, it was a sheer, vertical drop on to the pavement below. The wall was just wide enough for her feet to stand side by side, but there was no sloping roof to grab at. No second chances.

While the Hyena struggled to the front of the crowd, everyone watched her. But she still hadn't worked out how to speak to them. And already people were starting to get bored. They were glancing at Eddie, to see what the next entertainment would be.

She had to do something else, to keep their attention. And there was only one thing she could think of. The idea terrified her, but it was all there was.

Looking away from the crowd, she blanked them out of her mind and concentrated on what she was going to do. The world shrank round her. The people and the music disappeared. There was nothing but the bubble of space where she was facing the curved, narrow wall.

When she was quite steady, she went up on her hands and let her feet flop over, to balance her body. Then she began to climb, hands first, looking ahead for the next step and fighting the urge to glance down. All she could see was the top of the wall and the flaking paint that coloured the palms of her hands.

And the circus music went trumpeting on.

Now, the beautiful Miss Cindy will risk her life to bring

you a daredevil display of balance and courage! Watch her climb to the roof, without a safety net!! Thrill to her death-defying ridge walk!!! Marvel at her calmness . . .

At the top of the wall, the curve flattened to form the base of a triangle that pointed down. As she reached it, Ashley went up on her hands again and flipped her legs over the other way. Then she stood triumphantly, with her arms spread.

The applause was so loud that she could hear it, even above the music, but it didn't mean anything. Because Eddie was smiling at her. A small, triumphant smile. And she saw that she hadn't done anything brave or independent. Eddie's face said it all.

You see? You're just part of my show.

Then he waved his hand, dismissing her. It was finished. Her trick was over. He turned his back on the cinema and signalled to Sam, calling up another burst of flame. And the crowd turned too, following where he pointed.

From the roof of the car, Sam gave him a long look. Then she lifted her head to look up at Ashley. Their eyes met, but Ashley couldn't read that ice-blue stare. Not even when Sam raised the bottle, turning on the roof of the car as she opened her mouth. Not even when she tilted her head back and brought the torch towards it.

When it happened, it was a shock as sudden as the

burst of flame itself. As Sam breathed out, she jerked her head down sharply. Aiming her jet of fire at the top of Eddie's car. The flames roared and wrapped themselves round the loudspeaker, and there was an ugly, sizzling crackle. And a flash.

And then silence.

But it was only silent for a heartbeat, while Ashley realized what had happened. What Sam had done for her. Then she took in a huge breath and yelled into the silence, yelled, with every atom of breath in her lungs, every scrap of energy in her body.

'THE STALKER ISN'T MR GALT! HE'S INNOCENT! THE STALKER IS—!'

Her voice caught in her throat. What was Eddie's threat? *Say that outside this flat, and you'll be sorry. It's slander. You can't prove anything. The first whisper about stalking and you're in trouble.*

She was in enough trouble already. How could she cope with any more? But—someone had to say it. As long as people whispered and trembled and kept their mouths shut, Eddie would go on being the ringmaster. Someone had to take the risk.

'IT'S NOT MR GALT, IT'S—'

Her voice cracked again. But this time another voice broke in. A cold voice, as sharp as steel.

'Say that out loud, and you'll be sorry. It's slander. You can't prove anything. I've got solicitors!'

For a second, she thought it really was Eddie. Then she saw Sam bending down to haul Joe on to the roof of her car. He scrambled up beside her and for two or three seconds, he didn't say a word. He held the crowd in suspense, controlling them by the way he stood, by the tilt of his head and his arrogant, scornful stare.

Then he spoke again.

'No one puts me down, because you all jump when I crack the whip. I can do what I like on the Row, and no one touches me. Try it, and you'll suffer!'

He half-closed his eyes and pushed his face forward at Sam. Abruptly. Dangerously.

It was only a tiny movement. Ashley hadn't even noticed it particularly when Eddie did it. But the moment Joe mimicked it, she saw that it was Eddie to the life. Eddie blown up into a grotesque cartoon.

Everyone saw it. All round the car, people began to laugh, looking at Joe and then glancing sideways at the real Eddie, as if they were checking the resemblance. Joe played up to the laughter, picking up every little movement Eddie made and guying it, as if he had been practising for years.

Yes! Ashley thought, triumphantly. *Yes, yes, yes!* They'd done it. All of them together. They'd made people understand what Eddie was like and what he did. He was beaten!

She looked sideways, to see how he was taking it—and all her triumph fell away.

He was utterly still. There was no sign of anger on his face, no flinching. He didn't look beaten at all. He was standing in the middle of the crowd, silently watching Joe. Waiting for him to finish his turn.

His stillness started to affect people. One by one, they stopped laughing and edged away, until Eddie stood by himself in a circle of empty space. As the laughter disappeared, Joe's voice faltered, too. Finally, it died away and, for a second, the whole crowd seemed to hold its breath.

Then Eddie spoke, crisp and clear, into the silence.

'Oh dear, Joe,' he said. 'Oh dear, dear, *dear*. I thought you were my friend. But I was wrong, wasn't I?'

His voice was almost without expression, but Ashley had never felt such a sense of menace. Joe's pale clown-face turned dead white and his shoulders flagged as if he'd been beaten. Whatever Eddie was threatening him with, it didn't need to be spelt out. Ashley could feel the fear from where she stood.

And not only Joe's fear. The crowd faltered too. People began glancing at each other. Edging away from the cars. To Ashley, high on the cinema roof, it was like seeing Eddie tighten his grip on the Row. Fearless as a lion-tamer, he was facing down a whole crowd. Splitting the wild, dangerous pack that had

279

been ranged against him into separate, threatened individuals.

In another second, the whole crowd would have dispersed. But in the last, precarious instant, Ashley heard a soft footstep on the roof behind her.

And Tony Cavalieri leaned out of his window again, flapping his arms and yelling.

'Look out on the cinema! It's Eddie's men on the roof! Look out!'

Turning, automatically, Ashley saw Doug and another man only a few feet away, creeping past the ventilation shaft. They were hidden from the crowd by the high front wall, but she could see they were heading straight for her.

The shock of it was too much for her balance. She tried to keep her footing, but there was nothing to grab at. Her foot slipped and she knew she couldn't save herself.

As she fell, she heard the crowd roar.

LISA
She went off the top, and I started to scream. You can't help yourself. It's like a physical thing. Everyone was screaming and pushing backwards, so she wouldn't smash into them. And I was pushing back too, even though Ashley's one of my friends. I could feel Vikki doing it too, and Matt, and everyone. It was like a

disaster movie erupting suddenly in the middle of your real life. Everyone wanted to get out of the way.

Except the Hyena.

He didn't even hesitate. The moment she slipped, he raced forward, pushing people out of his way. He stood at the bottom of the wall with his arms held out for Ashley, as if he thought he could catch her.

Anyone could see it wouldn't work. There was no way he was going to be strong enough. But even though she went through his hands, he broke her fall. Instead of smashing straight into the tarmac, head first, she hit his shoulder and spun over. Her feet cracked him in the skull, which slowed her down even more and she hit the ground legs first, and crumpled and rolled.

You think I can't remember all that? I'm telling you—I could draw it, frame by frame. I dreamt the whole thing, over and over again, for weeks afterwards, and the worst of it wasn't the moment when she hit the ground. It was the next moment, when we all realized that we'd pulled back. We'd left her to die.

There was a horrible quietness.

Then someone said, 'It was Eddie's men!' and it swept over me like a great wave.

It was Eddie's fault! Everything. Eddie did it.

The whole crowd roared, out loud, and we started pushing towards Eddie's car. But he was too quick for us. He jumped into the car and drove off, going up on the pavement to get past the other cars. We chased him to the end of the Row, but he wasn't stopping. He'd have run over anyone who got in the way. He didn't even pull over to the left till he saw the ambulance coming for Ashley and the Hyena.

Of course, I never believed all that stuff about the Hyena stalking Ashley. I mean, anyone could see it was one of Eddie's little plots.

I can't think how he fooled people so long. Everyone always used to make out he was so good, fixing things for people, and that sort of stuff. The way they talked, you'd have thought he was some kind of fairy godmother.

Huh! Some fairy godmother. You should hear the tales that are going round the Row now that people know it's safe to tell. Every time I go into Annie's, there's someone else in there, letting another cat out of the bag, and they're always nasty little stories.

Mrs Macdonald's taking up a collection for the Hyena, and Annie puts up a notice every day, to say how he's doing. She says he's got so many flowers the hospital's going crazy.

If only he could see them . . .

30

Ashley opened her eyes and saw a white room. Hospital equipment. Flowers.

And Pauline in a wheelchair beside the bed.

Pauline took a quick breath and reached for her hand. 'Ashie? Can you hear me?'

'Of course,' Ashley tried to sit up. 'I'm perfectly—'

Then she lost the rest of the sentence and fell asleep.

The next time she came round, there were two nurses by her bed, busy with a drip. But Pauline was there too. Ashley blinked drowsily.

'The Hyena—'

'Mr Galt,' Pauline said.

'Yes, him. What happened? He hit me, or I kicked him, or something—'

'It was all my fault,' Pauline said. 'I should never have let you—'

Her face blurred, and Ashley let it go. She couldn't think about all that yet.

* * *

She couldn't think about anything much. For almost a week, she drifted in and out of sleep, without really remembering, trying to piece little bits together and giving up because the effort was exhausting. Faces flickered past her eyes—Janet, Vikki, Lisa—and she heard her voice mumbling to them. But when she looked at the flowers by her bed, and the cards and the grapes and the magazines, she couldn't remember who had brought them.

The only constant person was Pauline. She came every day in the wheelchair. Sometimes it was Janet and Frank who pushed her in, and sometimes it was another woman, with an unfamiliar face.

'That's Penny,' Pauline said, every time Ashley asked. 'She comes in to help me get up and go to bed. She's very nice. You'll like having her around.'

The first time she said it—and the second, and the third—the idea was so strange that Ashley forgot it. But gradually it stuck. Penny was coming in to look after her mother, and that was all right. She didn't have to worry. She could just let it happen.

'Janet kept on at me,' Pauline said. 'She said I had to get some help from the doctor and the Social Services. I didn't want to, but Tricia told me not to be an idiot.'

Tricia? There was something surprising about that, but Ashley couldn't work out what it was. She kept wondering about it, and forgetting, and then remembering again.

Until the morning when she woke up and found that her mind was completely clear. And she knew why she'd been surprised.

She sat up as far as she could. 'Did you say *Tricia* had been to see you?'

Pauline nodded. 'And Joe. It's helped me a lot, talking to them.'

'But what about Eddie? He said—'

Pauline hesitated, finding the words. 'People like Eddie have . . . lots of things going. They don't have to hang around if it gets difficult. He's moved on.'

'You mean . . . he's gone?' Ashley tried to get her brain round it. 'But what about his people? He told me he had people in every street.'

'Tricia says it's all changed. Phil's the one everybody's talking about now. Sam's going out with him, and Tricia says he's brilliant. He's really taking charge of things.'

Ashley felt strange. 'She used to think Eddie was brilliant.'

'Till he made fun of Sam, in front of everyone. And made Tricia laugh at it. That was his big mistake. She said it was really cruel.' Pauline squeezed Ashley's hand. 'Tricia's like me, you see. She thinks the world of her daughter.'

So that was what had swung it. After all the threats and the violence, it was a joke that had brought Eddie down.

And now Tricia was looking for a new fixer. Phil. Someone else to solve everyone's problems like magic. Was that better or worse?

Ashley concentrated on the things she could understand.

'At least Mr Galt's all right. Everyone knows he wasn't the stalker. He'll be fine now, won't he?'

'He—' Pauline's hand squeezed harder. 'Everyone thinks he's wonderful. They're calling him a hero in the Row.'

'So he doesn't mind any more? About me accusing him?'

'He—' Pauline stopped.

Even a day before, Ashley would have been too muzzy to wonder about that, but now her mind was working. 'There's something wrong, isn't there?' she said sharply. What she was thinking was too awful to say.

Pauline bit her lip. 'He's not dead. But he's still unconscious, and they're getting worried. His mother talked to him for an hour yesterday, to see if he'd respond to her voice, but it was no use.'

'So why don't they try someone else?'

'It's got to be a voice he'd recognize. Someone he cares about.'

Ashley linked her hands on top of the sheet and looked down at them. There was a dark bruise on the back of the right hand, turning an ugly yellow now. She thought about the Hyena dashing forward to catch her. About her feet, hitting the side of his head. And his bleak, unhappy face staring across the counter at her. *You mustn't be Cindy.*

'Can I go and talk to him?' she said.

It took two days to convince the doctors that it was worth organizing. Ashley was better, but she was still too weak to walk to the Neuro-Surgical Unit. One of the nurses had to take her in a wheelchair.

And when she was there, beside the Hyena's bed, she didn't know what to do. She sat helplessly, looking down at his face, which was even paler now. There was no mark on it, not a bruise or a scratch, but there was no sign of life, either. He was as still as a waxwork, pasty and middle-aged.

How could anything she said possibly make any difference to . . . that stranger?

'Don't worry,' the nurse said cheerfully. 'You haven't got to say anything earth-shaking. Just chat to him, the way you'd normally do.'

Oh, great, Ashley thought. *What do I say?*

How about: I'm sick of being chased and phoned and persecuted? Or: Why don't you stop stalking me?

'No need to be shy.' The Hyena's nurse joined in. 'Be yourself.'

But that was the trouble. If she'd been like Joe, with a hundred different voices to call on, she could have launched into a fantastic speech. If they'd given her spray-cans, she could have decorated the bare walls with black and yellow horses. She could even have turned cartwheels down the corridor, if it hadn't been for the plaster.

But she had nothing. She couldn't even run away.

Eddie had gone. The circus was over. There was nothing except the Hyena, lying there unconscious. And her voice.

She started to talk.

'The writing on your wall—it wasn't meant to be horrible. I know it sparked everything off, but I didn't do it to annoy you. I just wanted to climb up there and leave my mark. I wanted to be special . . . '

GEOFFREY

I can't say when I started hearing her voice, because in a way it was there all the time. I was dipping in and out of a grey mist, and her voice was whispering in my head. All sorts of things, coming back in a jumble.

LOOK! ARE YOU PROUD OF SENDING THAT TO ME?????...

... halfapoundofcookingonionsplease ...

THE STALKER ISN'T MR GALT! HE'S INNOCENT HE'S ... three cooking apples and a bag of sugar ...

Coming and going, round and round. I wanted to tell her it was all right, I wanted to say I understood, but my eyes wouldn't open and my voice wouldn't work. All the words in my head were hers.

... You're not my father. My father's dead ...

YOU'RE NOT THE STALKER ...

... pleasemaylhaveaboxofmatches ...

Her face kept drifting through my mind, like a ghost's face. Coming into focus and then blowing away. Not real, just a Cinderella in my head, twisting and dissolving and slipping away. I knew I had to catch the real Ashley—the one who shouted at me and painted on the wall—but whenever I tried to see her face, there was such a pain. Such a miserable, wrenching pain ...

... the writing ... wasn't meant to be horrible ...

... I just wanted to ... leave my mark ...

... I wanted to be special ...

The voice pushed its way in, until I couldn't believe it was just in my mind. But how could it be anywhere else? I'd seen her fall. I'd seen her hit the ground.

I meant to help her, the way I always wanted to. I meant to race in and catch her, like some kind of magician, flying to the rescue. But it was no use. She went through my hands like a thunderbolt, and I just keeled over. So when I heard her real voice—

I was scared to open my eyes in case I was making it up.

But you can't hide out in the dark for ever. If you do, you end up like Tony Cavalieri, wasting your life away. In the end, the real world's better, however bad it is. So I made myself look.

And she was there. She was sitting next to me, with half her hair cut off and a line of stitches across her scalp. She'd got stitches over one eyebrow, too, and her arm in plaster. The moment I saw all that, I knew she was real.

She'd survived without a magician.

But she didn't know what to say. I could see that in her face. She's only a child, after all.

So I helped her out with a little joke. 'Are there any pens around?' The words were croaky, because my voice was out of practice. 'It's my turn to do a bit of graffiti.'

She didn't get it at first. Not until one of the nurses

passed her a handful of felt tips. Then she grinned and held out her arm.

'You'd better leave a bit of room,' she said. 'My sisters'll kill me if they can't fit their names on.'

They can have the other side,' I said.

And I wrote my name along her arm, in three different colours. With shading.

Gillian Cross has been writing children's books for over thirty years. Before that, she took English degrees at Oxford and Sussex Universities, and she has had various jobs including working in a village bakery and being an assistant to a Member of Parliament. She is married with four children and lives in Dorset. Her hobbies include orienteering and playing the piano. She won the Carnegie Medal for *Wolf* and the Smarties Prize and the Whitbread Children's Novel Award for *The Great Elephant Chase*.

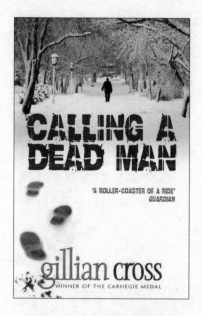

'A ROLLER-COASTER OF A RIDE'
GUARDIAN

gillian cross
WINNER OF THE CARNEGIE MEDAL

Isbn: 978-0-19-275588-9

How did John Cox die?

His sister Hayley thinks she knows, but she wants
to see the place where it happened. With John's friend
Annie she travels to Russia to visit the site of the
explosion that killed him.

But they soon realize that there is more to John's
death than meets the eye. And certain people are
desperate to keep them from finding out the truth.

Meanwhile, deep in the wastes of Siberia, a man with
no memory and a high fever stumbles out of the forest . . .

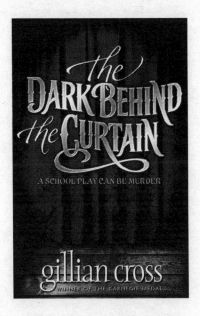

Isbn: 978-0-19-273163-0

'This play we're doing, it's not true, is it? I mean, there never was a Sweeney Todd who killed people?'

Jackus never wanted to be in the school play, but he didn't have much choice.

Now he sees that what's unfolding on-stage is more than just acting, more than just pretend. Strange things are happening. *Terrifying things*.

Ghostly footprints. Unexplained whispering. The touch of a cold hand in the shadows . . .

What has been woken by the play's dark words? Can Jackus stop it, or are the actors doomed to play out the tragedy to the bitter end?